MW01155526

# Windwood Farm

Copyright © 2014 by Rebecca Patrick-Howard

www.rebeccaphoward.net

Published by Mistletoe Press

All rights reserved. No part of this book may be reproduced, scanned, or distributed in any printed or electronic form without permission.

First Edition: April 2014

Printed in the United States of America

**For Joann Stepp**

# Chapter 1

She might depend on her eyes for most of her work, but it was her strong sense of smell that often accosted her first; the scent of death never fully left a place. As Taryn slowly drove down the long, loosely graveled driveway, taking careful observation of her surroundings, she was immediately hit by the overpowering aroma of devastation. It was an old scent and one covered up by others along the way but the closer she got to the house, the more quickly the layers peeled back until she was almost crying inside her old Dodge.

Fighting the urge to either burst into tears or throw up, she struggled to close off that part of her mind and ignore the stench and instead tried to focus on what was ahead. First impressions were always the most important to her in this job because that's when she saw the big picture. She would never fully get it again. Later, once she had grown accustomed to the place and her surroundings, she would pay careful attention to the details and the little nuances she often fell in love with. But it was the first look that usually hit her the hardest.

Taryn was not disappointed in the view. The low green hills and golden valleys spread out before her in all directions, giving her a panorama of beautiful countryside in the morning sun. She wasn't much of a morning person but she did have an appreciation for the light offered early in the day; the land was cast with a faint yellow glow then, as though the fields had been set on fire. It wouldn't happen again until sunset. The long driveway rambled off the main road and dipped down over a small rise and at the bottom of the hill there were woods she imagined led to the next farm. The trees were thick, dark and mysterious, adding to the ambience. She was glad that at least not everything was being developed around here, but how long would that last? Off in the distance, she saw the low rising buildings of town, creeping deliberately toward the farm in their urban sprawl, getting closer and closer as if they were ready to spring at any moment and capture the last remaining remnants of the farmland that lingered. Soon, it would be difficult to see any fields at all.

That was partly why she was there.

The grounds were well-kept with their sweet smelling grass thick and low and wild roses growing up wooden plank fences faded almost white in the summer sun. With her windows down, she could smell hay and the air was hot; sticky-sweet already and it was barely June. Someone was taking care of the property and not letting it get overgrown. That was good. Hopefully it meant there wouldn't be too many snakes. She didn't do snakes.

The barns and smaller outbuildings caught her eye before the house. They were in disrepair, but stood solidly despite missing several key structural frames. A chicken coop had seen better days and was lopsided, but it was trying. She applauded its tenacity. The barn looked downright sturdy. She recalled seeing a leaning barn outside of Cleveland that rivaled the tower in Pisa, and this barn didn't look as if it were going anywhere anytime soon, either. It was weathered and bleached in the sun, and several boards were missing, but she could easily imagine it filled with equipment and horses, their hooves beating on the dirt floor, ready to get the morning started. She loved exploring barns, even the unsafe ones. Perhaps because she'd grown up in the city, she'd always felt a calling for the countryside and enjoyed herself whenever she was in it.

The house itself was set before her, peeking stoically out from behind two overgrown oak trees, their branches reaching up into the sky as if in prayer and their leaves full, almost overpowering the house.

It was a timeworn stone structure, built in 1849, with an addition thoughtlessly tacked on the back. That part was painted a dingy white, the paint flaked off through the years, leaving it pock-marked and naked. Nobody ever bothered to fix it, that she could tell. Indeed, the house hadn't been lived in since the 1930s for reasons that hadn't yet been explained to her.

Dense, feminine, ivy with delicate fingers curved her nails around the front doors but it didn't really matter since the doors were nailed shut with thick, ugly wooden planks that peeked grotesquely through the vines.

The fact that the house was constructed of stone was part of what set it apart from other houses built during the same era; the fact that the architect had gone on to achieve some critical acclaim was another. A young man when he designed this house, he went on to design several more in Washington, D.C. and New York City and then won the A1A Gold Medal, awarded by the American Institutes of Architects. His designs appeared in textbooks today across the country. The local historical society was proud of this fact, and rightly so. And, of course, it *was* a fine-looking house. Taryn was immediately in love with it, the same way she fell in love with most older homes that were in disrepair and needed a little love, despite the bad feelings she'd had when she'd first turned down the drive.

Unfortunately, although the house was solid and, in her mind, easily fixable (all old buildings were worth preserving in Taryn's mind), a couple of rooms on the front had collapsed years ago and now lay in a rumpled heap on the sunny grass.

Parking her old Dodge in front, she got out with her Nikon (affectionately named Miss Dixie) slung over her shoulder and began walking around, taking shots when it suited her. She was paid to paint, but she always started with photographs of her subject. Not only did they help jog her memory later, but it was also how she got to know her surroundings. She had a special relationship with her camera and through the viewfinder, she saw architectural details she might otherwise miss. Miss Dixie was often her eyes and picked up on things that Taryn herself sometimes missed. They were a team.

Goosebumps dotted her arms and thighs as she walked through the grass. As she'd sprained her ankle once in a gopher hole while walking backward trying to get a shot of a gable, she was now mindful of any critters or mole holes that might be lurking. She knew she needed to pull herself together. The initial feeling she got when she first pulled into the driveway was waning and she tried hard to ignore it further. Her connection with the properties she worked with was both her strongest asset and her weakest link. She felt for old houses and buildings the way many people felt for animals and children. In some ways, the old houses she became attached to *were* her children, or at least her foster kids for a little while. Taryn didn't understand how anyone couldn't love these remnants from the past with their heartbreaking beauty and grace. And when they were abandoned and neglected, they were almost even more beautiful to her. They all had pasts and stories to her; sometimes, she let herself become close to them before she even got to know them. For someone who wasn't much of a romantic when it came to men, she had no qualms when it came to love at first sight with buildings.

For whatever reason, this house and farm tugged at her through the photographs the Stokes County Historical Society sent her before she'd even had the chance to see it in person. Now, seeing it in person and finding it sadly neglected, this beautiful farm had taken her a little by surprise. And it *had* been a long drive up from Tennessee. That could be the only plausible explanation for the sudden emotions she'd experienced when she'd entered the property.

She hoped.

Taryn didn't spook easily but she did pick up on the past. It's what made her good at her job: the ability to empathize with her subjects. *It's not* real *death you're sensing,* she told herself as she walked around, *it's the death of this grand house.*

It didn't matter that she'd only been commissioned to paint the front of the house: She would take photos inside and out of the entire thing. She'd even spend time photographing the surrounding farm and outbuildings. Taryn believed that in order to paint anything, you must know it completely. Although the back door might not be in her finished painting, it didn't mean it wasn't important. She had to understand how it fit into the overall structure. Her degree in Historical Preservation taught her that everything about the building (and in this case, the entire farm) was important. Her degree in Art helped taught her appreciation of the details. Her own sense of curiosity and adventure filled in the rest.

The owner, Reagan Jones, would meet her there tomorrow and show her around, but she'd had a hankering to get on the road and arrived a day earlier than expected, wanting to see it for herself. She worked best without an audience.

The scent was still there, picking at the edge of her mind, but she ignored it. It would come and go as long as she was there and learning to push it down was something she'd perfected over the years. She wasn't there to talk or think about death; she was there to bring a moment of the past to life again.

The house appeared to be structurally sound as far as she could tell. She'd worked with enough architects to know what to look for, and a quick tour of the cellar didn't give any indication that the floors might collapse under her should she decide to walk around upstairs. However, the wolf spiders down there were more than enough to satisfy her curiosity of that particular part of the house. (She didn't really do spiders, either.)

It wasn't the most beautiful house she'd ever seen, but the stone frame made it visually interesting and the fluttering torn curtains on the second floor made her sad. The worst part of her job was in knowing that many of the structures she painted would be demolished and gone soon after she left, but it gave her solace to know at least someone cared enough to document their existence. Without that, she wouldn't have a job.

A stroll around the back showed her the addition; a jolting white plank work that she was sure embarrassed the original home. She imagined buildings had memories and feelings and held onto them the same way people did, although this wasn't something she normally shared with people she didn't know (or most she *did)*. Most people might find this romanticism a little nutty. She had just turned thirty, but she'd learned a long time ago that not everyone shared her sentiments when it came to inanimate objects.

Strangely enough, considering the fact the front doors were so tightly bound, the back door was standing wide open. The screen door had fallen off its hinges and lay across the grass where dandelions grew through the tears and holes. She could see all the way into what appeared to be a darkened kitchen and through the small window on the other side of the room, which was not boarded up like the other windows.

She stood there on the wooden steps, a little rotted through but they still held her, and weighed her options. Should she invite herself in? After all, she was hired to do a job here, although, to be fair, it wasn't by the owner himself but by the Stokes County

Historical Society. (She figured they must've come into some grant money to afford her fees.)

She wasn't exactly a stranger when it came to inviting herself into empty, deserted places. She'd been known to scale a fence or two and climbing into windows of abandoned houses was not unheard of back when she was younger and more nimble. But she wasn't the spring chicken she once was and here she felt as though there were eyes on her, watching each move she made and the feeling was an uncomfortable one. A quick look around revealed hers was the only vehicle for as far as she could see, but Taryn nevertheless got the feeling she wasn't alone.

However, the sense of adventure finally won out.

Figuring that asking for forgiveness was always easier than asking for permission, she decided to give it a go and continue her exploration. Gently, she stepped up onto the cracked cement landing and peered into the darkened doorway. A peek into the shadowy room confirmed that it was a kitchen. An old tin coffee pot still set on the ancient stove and a round table was covered by a plastic red checkered table cloth that was starting to mildew. There were bird and rodent droppings all over it, and most of it was black but the pattern was still visible through the stains and debris. Some tin cans littered the table and counters, as if someone had recently walked away from them.

"Hello!" she called into the house. She was met with silence.

Taking a chance, she crossed over the frame and entered the house.

Despite the warm summer morning, the house was cool; almost cold. The sense that she was an intruder was amplified by the objects that littered the room. The plates, the utensils, the tablecloth, the coffee pot—it was as if someone had just gotten up and left. That is, if they had left twenty years ago or more.

A small door led from the kitchen into what she assumed was a dining room and she walked toward it, her ears tuned into the sounds of the house. She heard nothing. The dining room held an old metal table but was otherwise bare, save for a couple of empty boxes and some dated calendars on the wall. A living room awaited her on the other side. She stopped in the door frame and held her breath, listening. She had grown accustomed to working alone in deserted places and was usually able to tell whether or not anyone was nearby simply by listening and taking stock of her surroundings. Sometimes, the simple change of air currents was enough. This time, the house was deathly still. Letting out her breath, she continued on into the living room.

The moment she crossed the door, she held her breath again, but this time subconsciously. Second by second, the air thickened around her, a feeling of pressure increased on her chest and back, and cold chills raced down her shoulders to her fingertips. Her legs nearly buckled under her from the shock. To steady herself, she placed her left hand on the wall and felt crumbling paper under her fingers. It felt like dead flesh decaying beneath her touch and she quickly snatched her hand away and wiped it on her jeans. "Get a grip, dummy," she mumbled to herself. She was a pro at giving herself pep talks. She might be used to exploring old places, and might have even been used to picking up on scents and energy, but that didn't mean she didn't get scared. She was no fool.

The room was dark, darker than the kitchen, and the one long pale ray of light that filtered in through the boarded up windows showed a dilapidated couch and a coffee table turned on its end. The rug was old and moth-eaten, with rodent droppings speckling its once green and red design. The furniture was at least forty years old, if she were to guess, at least some of it. Other pieces were even older. The house had been empty for a very, very long time. There was nothing menacing about the room itself or the objects it contained, but the air...the air. It was stifling.

Taryn took another step forward and it hit her again, the wave of power and the horrible scent. Wrapping her arms tightly around herself, an old habit of self-defense, she slowly made her way toward the center of the room. It felt like walking through molasses, every step taking more effort than the last. Moving through the darkness didn't feel real and for a fleeting moment, she wondered if perhaps she had fallen asleep in her car while she was driving and was dreaming. She stood in the center, slowly turning around and around, and saw nothing out of the ordinary. The air was still without even the sound of mice in the walls, and yet she felt as if she'd entered a cyclone. A dull roar started first in her left ear and then in her right and as pressure filled her head she got the overwhelming feeling she was chest deep in water, unable to properly catch her breath.

*I'm not wanted here*, she thought to herself and the cold air rippled as if her inner voice was heard and the house was agreeing with her.

Giving into another habit, she quickly turned on Miss Dixie and began snapping pictures around the room. The brief flashes of light were soothing and the sound of the shutter hypnotic. She always felt less alone when her camera was on. It had become a friend over the years, so much so that she continued to get it fixed rather than purchase a new one. The pressure slowly eased off her chest and back and the roar stopped as the camera clicked and flashed. Soon, it was just a gloomy living room again.

Gathering new courage again with her camera on, she decided against making a run for the back door. That didn't mean she didn't head for it at a quick pace, however. Another room was visible through the doorway in front of her and there were two staircases on either side of the room that she assumed led to bedrooms, but instead of continuing on, she turned and went back to the kitchen, snapping pictures as she went. The moment she stepped into the brighter light, the feeling of coldness left her, as did the dread.

Back outside, Taryn let out a huge exhale and a nervous laugh as she turned and faced the house again. "What the *hell* was what?" she asked aloud, accusingly, as she glared at the stone walls.

Sighing, Taryn walked back to her car, this time with a quicker step. For once, she was afraid she might have encountered a house that wasn't particularly pleased at her presence. She was going to have to win it over.

Taryn checked into her hotel room, a nondescript chain with five stories that looked like every other place she'd ever stayed in, and went through her file on the house on Snowden Lane. Windwood Farm, it had been called, and that's what she aimed to title her painting and call it from here on out.

A purposeless reality show on VH-1 (her biggest vice, although not her only one) played softly in the background, mostly for company. She knew it might cost her some brain cells, but it somehow mollified her to see rock stars she had once idolized stooping to the level of looking for dates on television. Everyone was apparently going through a dry spell.

What she'd felt at the house unnerved her. Okay, who was she fooling, it had *scared* her. But she didn't have the luxury of giving into those fears. Last month, her car broke down and she'd needed a new transmission. Between that and some dental work back in the spring, her meager savings were cleared out. Lots of offers had come through, but they just barely covered the bills. Taryn was in financial trouble, hardly able to do more than make her credit card payments and rent. Everyone wanted her; nobody wanted to pay much. She *needed* this job. Without it, she might end up on the street. Whatever was in the house would learn to live with the fact that they were going to be stuck together for the next month or so. Besides, she didn't really believe in ghosts and bad vibes couldn't kill her.

She didn't have much history on the place other than dates. She knew a little bit about it from her correspondence with the president of the historical society, though. The first owner had the home built and lived there until 1902. The second owner, and the last person to really live there, bought it in 1903 and lived there until 1934. Although the next owner bought it right away and apparently moved furniture in from the looks of things, it was never truly lived in again, although the land was farmed. The house was sold again in the 1970s. The current owner was the son of the last owner. He inherited the house from his father. That was all Taryn knew. For all intents and purposes, despite the addition and the furniture inside, the house had been empty since 1934 according to her correspondence.

She was curious about what had happened to the house, but Taryn wasn't there to make judgments on the events that occurred during the house's lifespan, at least not out loud. She would probably judge them eventually because, well, she was human. In Taryn's occupation, it was more important that she painted the structures she saw as they would have been in their glory days, before the devastation they were currently facing. She was to see through their destruction and find remnants of their former splendor and life and try to capture that in paint for future preservation. Before they were demolished. Or, in some rare cases, to help with their restoration. It was true, anyone was capable of coming in and taking pictures of their house or property, even the owners themselves, but what she offered was something special.

Taryn's talent was in seeing things and places the way they once were and then showing that in her paintings through creativity and a certain amount of sensitivity. Her degree and studies of historical architecture helped her look at even the most dilapidated of places and restructure them in her paintings, sometimes the only complete version of the building her clients had ever seen. She'd been called in to paint houses that had little more than the columns still standing and she'd been able to give the clients beautiful (their word, not hers, she wasn't *that* narcissistic) renderings of their ancestral homes complete with second floor, attic, and gazebo.

It was true, of course, that most of the places she was hired to capture were in shambles, which made her job a lot harder. This one, however, still looked secure from the outside. Painting it would take a little imagination on her part, since part of it had crumbled, although she had a feeling she would still need to use sensitivity.

Sometimes that sensitivity could get her in trouble. It was one thing to use your imagination to visualize the way a grand staircase used to look with its polished oak and sparkling crystal chandelier above it. It was another thing to actually *see* it. And sometimes, just sometimes, she thought she could. If she closed her eyes hard enough, she imagined and even *saw* what the place would have looked like before time and neglect set in. She even dreamed about the places she worked in, sometimes seeing them fully furnished and ready for balls or weddings or decorated for the holidays.

Occasionally, she became so wrapped up in a place she became attached to it and invested in it, and sometimes it was hard to move away from those feelings once the job ended. She'd become part of more than one house.  It was an occupational hazard. Of course, she wanted to purchase every single one she fell in love with. But nobody paid her that well.

# Chapter 2

Reagan Jones was an energetic young man, no more than thirty, with a developer's eye and a politician's smile. Taryn had met many men like him over the years, those who thirsted for real estate development and hated to see an empty field as much as some people hated to see strip malls. This was the first time she'd met one quite so young, however.

He hopped out of his SUV with a big smile and had her walking around the property again in no time, pointing out landmarks and explaining his future plans for the area. "It's all going to be a subdivision," he said hurriedly. "But not one of those with all the houses looking the same. Each house will have at least one acre, maybe two if they want to purchase more. It will be like having a mini farm!"

*It wouldn't be* anything *like having a mini farm*, Taryn thought to herself, but she smiled pleasantly. He was, for the time being, sort of her boss. "I'm going to have to get a little more information about the property and was hoping you could answer some questions for me."

"Well, I can surely try," he said seriously, his large hazel eyes growing wide. He had a slight paunch and some of his features were a little large for his small face, but he wasn't an unattractive man and Taryn was receiving a warm vibe from him, despite his enthusiasm for tearing down a large, seemingly structurally sound, and beautiful home. He spoke with an easy drawl but even with his polished look and laid-back style (he wore loafers and jeans) he was calculating. She suspected that he was one of those men whom everyone liked, even when they were being bulldozed. "I don't rightly know a whole lot about it. It belonged to my daddy who bought it from the third owner. It got passed down to me because I'm an only child. My daddy owned a lot of properties around here. Nobody's lived in it since the thirties. My daddy was the oldest son, his other brothers died in the war, and he lived there on the property for about a year and then gave it up. Lived in a camper. Never used the house at all. Just storage, mostly. After he built our house he just used the barn here. The other owners before him didn't really live in it at all. Maybe a few nights here and there. Nobody's lived in it permanently, as far as I know, since 1934."

"It looks like it," Taryn mumbled. "I'm sorry, but I stopped here yesterday and walked around a bit. I went inside because it was open and for a minute I was startled and thought someone might be staying here. It looks lived in."

"Yeah," Reagan laughed. "It does that to you. Me? I don't like to go in there unless I have to. My wife won't go in at all. Says it gives her the willies. Local kids don't even bother it. You won't find anyone sneaking in there to smoke or fool around. I could leave the door open year round and not a soul would touch it."

Taryn must have looked skeptical because he laughed. "What? You don't believe in ghosts? And I thought your job was seeing things that aren't there. Isn't that another way of seeing ghosts?"

Taryn shrugged. "I chalk it up to having a good imagination. And no, I've never seen a ghost. I don't think I believe in them. Not really."

Reagan laughed and patted her shoulder. "Well, maybe that's why you haven't seen them."

"I think I believe in something," Taryn smiled. "I just don't know what yet."

"Stick around," Reagan laughed. "Just stick around. You will!"

Considering her occupation, people were always asking her if she ever saw any ghosts. But what could she tell them? That she always felt the presence of something but could never quite put her finger on what it was? She liked to think of her talent as a kind of sensitivity to leftover energy. Like the photographs she took, she thought places held memories and figured she was tuned into those, or something to that effect. Occasionally, she did stumble across a spooky place that made her feel uncomfortable, like the old mental hospital in Danvers, Massachusetts (or that Victorian monstrosity that had her seeing shadows and questioning her sanity a few times), but usually after being in it for a couple of days she was able to get past whatever she felt and work well within the environment. As long as she remembered that what she was seeing and feeling was nothing more than a memory or hologram she kept the ill feelings at bay.

Yesterday had been unnerving, and she hadn't slept well the night before, but new places always did that to her. Besides, it was possible that she had simply been tired and had imagined what she felt. Old houses had personalities and perhaps this one's was just a little strong. It didn't mean that she slept any easier that night, however.

After a quick trip around the exterior of the house, Reagan went back to the kitchen door Taryn had entered the day before. "This is about the only way you can get in and out. Front's all boarded up. I can take the boards down if it will help with the doors and stuff."

"It would help, actually, especially if the original door is still there behind the planks. Why do you have them boarded up if you say people won't come in here?"

"Well, when I first got the house, I didn't know that. Had the whole thing boarded up. When I saw nobody was going to bother it, I took them down in the back. I like to come in and check on things from time to time...not often though," he added.

The kitchen looked the same, vacant and unused, but was set for a breakfast scene that was never going to happen. On closer inspection, the tin cans had obviously been there for a long time, possibly twenty years or more.

Reagan took her into a room off the kitchen she hadn't seen the day before. It was a small, narrow room with a single bed and a battered dresser. Both were in bad shape. A man's work clothes were scattered about the floor and hangers were tossed carelessly about. It appeared someone left in a hurry. The clothes didn't give the impression to be that far out of style, and Taryn looked at them in confusion. "Was somebody staying here?"

"Yeah. Two summers ago, we decided to fix this place up, me and my wife. Thought we could add on to it, it doesn't have but two bedrooms upstairs and we've got three kids, and make it real nice again. I heard it used to be a real beauty. So we brought this guy in to pack up the good stuff and haul out the junk. Do some of the landscaping, too. Told him he could stay here while he did it, cause we knew it would take a couple of months.

"Well, he stays for about a week and then ups and leaves. Tacks a note on my front door saying that he can't stay no more and he's gotta be getting back to Indiana, to home. So I call him and ask him if he wants me to send him his clothes and such that he left behind and he says no, he don't need a thing. Beat all I ever seen." Reagan shook his head at the memory and laughed. "I came in here and looked around and found his wallet, full of money. I mailed that to him. Must've been in a hurry. I'm gonna put in a call to the Salvation Army and see if they can use any of this furniture. My wife has everything at home the way she wants it and doesn't want me bringing anything else in to mess it up."

Taryn smiled pleasantly and gave a nod, hoping it looked to be in encouragement.

The jovial smile never left Reagan's face. "You'll understand that better if you ever meet the missus. She's real particular about certain things."

"If there are two bedrooms upstairs, why didn't he sleep up there?"

Reagan shrugged, and turned back to the kitchen. "Don't know. Might make more sense when you see one of them, though.

Came in here that first day and looked around and then said he'd rather sleep down here. I hauled in a bed from our storage unit. He said that was fine."

"So after that, you decided not to fix it up?"

"No, we still thought we might. My wife came over a few times and worked outside. Still keeps some gardening tools here because the shed here is bigger. We live in a subdivision I developed myself and only have but one outbuilding to make room for the swing set and swimming pool. Came in with some boxes—you'll see them in the living room—and tried to pack up some stuff herself. Then she said she didn't like it anymore and wasn't going to come back by herself. She got spooked. That was the end of that."

They were heading toward the living room, and her breath caught. She hoped that whatever she felt before was nothing but the result of a long day of driving because she was damned if she was going to look like a fool in front of him. The scent that accosted her on her first visit was already less potent than before. But when they stepped across the doorway, she was still surprised. Nothing. Not even a chill passed over her skin. *Maybe it had just been an illusion*, she told herself.

"This here was the dining room," Reagan continued. "My daddy was going to use it as a living area himself. Must've been easier to heat than the living room and the parlor. I don't know. There was an old couch in here. We already hauled it away."

"Was he related to the other owner? Your dad, I mean?"

"Oh, no. He bought it at auction. And that guy did, too. None of us knew Robert Bowen, the one who lived here longest."

"Did Robert live here alone?" The personal background was probably more helpful to Taryn than any other research she could have done. Sure, she had her design books back in her room and a history of the area, but it was the people who made the house and figuring out how they lived put it all into perspective.

Reagan shook his head and went on into the adjoining room. "No. Well, at the end he did. Died of a heart attack or something or other. In the beginning he was married. She died around five years into the marriage. One of those old-timey diseases that nobody gets anymore. I can't remember what it's called. Sorry. Don't know much about her. They had a daughter but she died, too. That I do know. After that, he lived alone."

"How did he make his money? And what did he do through the Depression? Or was this area not hit very hard?"

"Oh, this area was hit. Kentucky was hit just as hard as anyplace else, though the smaller towns didn't get all of them riots and stuff cause they was fairly small to begin with and employment had always been bad around here. But it got hit. No, he made his money from tobacco, same as a lot of people here. Even in a Depression, people gotta smoke."

*So he was a farmer*, Taryn made a mental note. And this wasn't a grand house inside, although it was large, so he probably did at least some of the work himself. She wondered when the wife and daughter died. Local records would show that, if she decided it was important enough to know. It might not be. She had a lot to work with already. She was already starting to get to know the house and too much more might muddle things up. But sometimes her curiosity got the best of her. It was funny how stepping through the doors of a place could instantly start her wheels turning.

The living room was large as well. She hadn't noticed before. She'd been too caught up in trying to figure out what was going on. It was the front room, and a glance at the boarded up door gave Taryn faint chills. She brushed them off by telling herself the boards simply blocked out the natural light and made the room unusually dark. That was enough to give anyone the creeps.

Reagan, as if reading her mind, chuckled. "Guess it does make the place spooky. Sorry it's so dark in here. I'll get those taken down. Won't be able to take any pictures if you can barely see your hand in front of your face. I read your website. I know you like to take pictures first," he said at her bemused expression.

"That's okay," she shrugged. "I don't mind being cyber stalked."

"This here was the living room. Nothing left in here anymore except the fireplaces. And some old furniture, of course. When Dad died, we took most of the good furniture, especially from these front rooms. Sold anything we could. Nothing really in here, though. Never was. Seems like that's as far as they got though because as you saw from the kitchen and as you'll see from the upstairs, everything's still left up there from when Robert and his family lived here in the 20s and 30s. Interesting thing about this room is the two staircases. See?"

Taryn looked around and indeed, saw the two sturdy wooden staircases in the two corners of the room. "Where do they go?"

"One goes up to one bedroom and one goes to the other. Oddest thing I've ever seen. You'd think maybe they was added separately but they weren't. House was built at the same time except for the back. After the Bowens died off, nobody ever really used the place. Not for long anyway. Just farmed the land."

Taryn nodded absently and then wandered over to the nearest staircase and studied it. It was simple and sturdy, but not ornate. Something one might find in a farmhouse. A ray of pale light fell down through the steps, suggesting there might be a window upstairs. The fireplace mantle *was* decorative, however, with carvings and decorations adorning it. Why spend money on one and not the other?

Taryn was so intent on her musings she didn't notice when Reagan wandered out of one room and into the next. Suddenly, a wave of cold air blasted her and she staggered, caught off-guard. Cold needles pricked her skin and as she brought her arms up to cross in front of her protectively, the room began to swim. As if seeing it through a wave of water, she blinked her eyes, and watched as murky shadows began to manifest. Scared at first, she couldn't help but be a little intrigued as well, and she experimentally reached out her hand to touch a nearby passing shape. As her fingers made contact, a flash of lightning struck them. "Ouch!" she cried out in pain.

"You okay in there?" Reagan's voice was faint, as if coming from a well, with a slight echo. She could hear his footsteps coming toward her and she closed her eyes again. When she opened them, he was standing before her and the room was once again empty.

"Sorry, splinter," she tried to laugh. "From the staircase."

A puzzled look flickered across his face and then it was gone. "You gotta be careful in here," he shrugged. "This place is falling apart and you don't know what all you can get into. The floor's sound as a rock but I don't keep insurance on it. I should, but I don't. So don't get hurt and sue me." He flashed her a million dollar smile and winked. Taryn smiled back.

With shaking legs that belied her outward appearance, Taryn tried to compose herself. *Am I losing my mind?* she asked herself worriedly. *What the hell is going on in here?* Reagan appeared easy and comfortable; an owner simply walking through the rooms of a house he had no use for. How was it possible he didn't feel something a little off? Or did he?

The next room, a smaller parlor, was similar to the front room and also boasted a fireplace, this one missing a mantle. Otherwise, the room was dark and bare, with little to distinguish it from any number of empty rooms Taryn had seen in other homes from the same time period. The darkness was throwing Taryn off, but she wasn't surprised Reagan had boarded the place up; this was definitely the kind of place that teenagers and rounders liked to use for a party pad, except for the fact that Reagan said he didn't have a problem with that.

"You wanna go upstairs?" His voice echoed and bounced off the walls, a lonely and hollow sound in the darkness.

Taryn nodded and they began their ascent up the plain staircase. "Do you think anyone was ever going to replace these staircases with something more permanent and just never got around to it?"

Reagan shook his head. "Don't know. Kind of ugly for the house, huh?"

They both laughed.

"Still here though," he added. "So many of these get vandalized and ripped apart. Guess nobody wanted this one. My uncle sold some of the mantles. My daddy runned an antique store for years. People like those old mantles. Them and the bannisters are usually the first things to get ripped out of these old houses. But not this one. Easy to see why."

It was a surprise to find that the stairs opened up right into the bedroom. No hallway, no sitting area, nothing. An unusual lack of privacy for the time period, Taryn noted, especially since houses built in the mid-nineteenth century were so fond of their doors. It made conserving heat easier since you could always shut off rooms you weren't using but in today's designs, people were all about open concepts and wide-open spaces. Those wide-open spaces sometimes made Taryn feel a little claustrophobic. She liked her doors and actual rooms that had specific purposes.

Mysteriously enough, if the living room and parlor were mostly empty and bare of odds and ends from the past, this room looked as if it had just been abandoned the day before. The paint on the old white wrought iron metal bed might have been peeling and the mattress moldy, but it was pushed to the window where dainty lace curtains still fluttered in the morning breeze. They were moth-eaten and dusty, but still fairly intact except for a few tears here and there. Mildewed sheets were thrown haphazardly across the bed and fell onto the floor, as if someone just recently pushed them aside. A featherbed was smoothed over the frame and a few loose feathers drifted in the air, aroused by the air currents Taryn and Reagan disturbed. A broken rocking chair sat in the corner of the room, staring into the middle of the floor, as if keeping watch.

A lone waterfall dresser was pushed against the far side of the wall and it was to this that Taryn's attention was drawn to the most. The drawers were all gaping, revealing articles of clothing that could have been slips or nightgowns. A small oak jewelry box set atop the dresser and it was open as well, displaying rings, cameos, and necklaces. Some of them, even to Taryn's fairly untrained eye, appeared to be the real deal. A porcelain china doll was lying on its side, its once fine face smashed into pieces. A set of keys rested beside it: heavy, masculine skeleton keys that appeared out of place in the otherwise feminine room. The entire dresser looked as if someone just recently went through it in a hurry, maybe looking for something.

Reagan was watching her, his long arms folded causally across his chest, his polo shirt and jeans looking out of place. Taryn felt as if both of them were standing in the midst of a movie set. She was confused. "So you say that people don't come in here and go through things?"

"That's right," he replied with a faint smile on his face. He had seen all of this before and was watching her with amusement, waiting for her reaction.

"Well, it looks like someone came in and went through this room," she muttered as she walked over to the dresser and ran her hand over the keys. They were cold and heavy under her fingers.

"Wellll...not exactly. You see, this bedroom has been like this for as long as I can remember."

Taryn turned and looked at him, confused. "What do you mean?"

"It's *always* looked like this. I'm thirty-five years old and it's been this way since I was a baby, probably before. The downstairs? Yeah, kids came and went down there some. But something kept them from going any further. Back in the 70s, my daddy said he ran a few off, some who had taken some silver and things from the dining room. But not in years. My wife, she come up here once and tried to clean. Pushed those drawers closed, put that jewelry back into the box, picked up those papers on the floor, even tried to make the bed. Said that it looking like this all the time bothered her. Then she went back downstairs for a little while. Heard some noises here. When she came back up, it looked

28

just the same as it did before. This room just don't want to be touched."

# Chapter 3

Taryn and Reagan sat on the front steps of the old house, looking out over the fields and gravel lane. "It's in remarkably good condition. I mean, to have been vacant for, what, how many years? Unbelievable." She wasn't sure if she was really going to believe that the house kept people from messing with it, but she was ready to admit there was something special about it.

Reagan nodded. "Part of that is because it's stone. Part of it because we've kept it covered and those old trees right here keep it shaded. I've patched the roof up over the years and there's not a drop of water that can get into the house. It will come into the cellar, of course, and the whole thing smells musty. I'm sure if we knock out some of those walls we're gonna find black mold up to our ears, but it *is* still standing."

Making both physical and mental notes while Reagan talked, now she stopped. "So why do it now? Why tear it down? Why not build around it? Restore it?" It really did break her heart to think of something that had stood there for so long to be knocked over in the name of a subdivision and "progress."

"I don't have the money. People look at me and think I do, but I don't. I borrow it, same as everybody else does. I have debts, too. I had a guy look at it once. He said it would cost as much to fix it as it would to build a new one. The foundation is fair, as far as we know, but you're looking at a house that was built two centuries ago and hasn't been updated since. No plumbing, no electric, weak floors, needs a new roof...It's just not my project. And then there's the other thing...nobody here would want to live in it. Would take an outsider. Fact is, if it wasn't for the Stokes County Historical Society throwing a fit over it, I wouldn't have even called you here to do your thing to it. No offense or nothing," he added hurriedly.

Taryn nodded. That was usually the case—the owners rarely took their own initiative in these matters. She was used to it. But at least Reagan was honest about it. But what had he meant about nobody from there not wanting to live in it?

"Well, I hate to see it go, but then I hate to see all old houses go. It's yours and you can do what you want with it. I can get started this evening," she said as she stood up and dusted off her pants. "I like the sunset light the best, next to early morning. But I'm not really a morning person. Take me about three weeks finish, maybe a little longer. I'll say five weeks to be on the safe side."

"No worries," Reagan smiled. "We don't plan on doing anything with it until the end of summer. I've got my hands full with some other business as it is. Feel free to poke around and do what you have to do. Just don't get hurt."

"Thanks. I usually spend the first few days just kind of getting acquainted with the place, looking around, doing some sketches and photographs."

Reagan shrugged. "However you have to work. My wife? She's a photographer too. Mostly kids. You do a lot of houses like this?"

"Not so much anymore," Taryn answered quickly. "Mostly museums and historical sites. I don't do a lot of private homes anymore. This one...called to me, I guess you could say. Or else the ladies at the historical society were pretty persistent."

Reagan smiled. "Well, they are that, I can attest."

"I have my cell on me if you need anything," she said as she started toward her car.

"Oh," Reagan called after her. "You won't need it. Can't get a signal out here. The company says there's coverage but this must be a dead zone."

When the Stokes County Historical Society first approached Taryn about the job, she was reluctant. She didn't do jobs associated with many private homes anymore. This was for reasons of her own, but mostly because the owners liked to nose around and make her nervous and she enjoyed having free run of the place. It had taken some pleading on their part for her to accept this one, and she did so only after they assured her it was vacant and nobody would bother her. And, of course, once they assured her that they could actually afford her. She hated to be petty about the money thing, but she really did need it.

It was the name that drew her to the house from the beginning: Windwood. It didn't take much to understand where it came from, either. With the house's position atop the ridge the wind was certainly strong enough to blow you over if you didn't watch your step. She was going to have to weigh her easel down and clamp her canvas to it. Luckily, the tall maple and oak trees blocked the worst of the wind. She assumed there had once been more woods than what were presently visible, but the ones she could see were thick and dark and almost romantic with their position at the foot of the valley.

She'd been in constant contact with the president and secretary of the Stokes County Historical Society for almost six weeks and she knew the time was coming when she'd have to go over and meet the women (and presumably men) who were a part of it, especially since they were technically her employers. But so far she'd been engrossed with getting acquainted with the house and meeting Reagan, the rightful owner anyway.

They hadn't told her anything about the property itself, just the dates of construction and architectural features she might find interesting. That was enough for her at the time. She'd especially enjoyed the pictures they sent her of the property. Looking back, she'd had no idea that photographs were about to become so important.

The house and surrounding farm certainly appeared ordinary enough in the images they'd sent her; maybe a little sad and forgotten, but those were the kinds of places that drew her.

Taryn started her degree program when she was eighteen, but she'd started her career much earlier. Since Matt first got his license at age sixteen, he had driven them around to deserted houses and buildings so she could "explore" (a nicer word than breaking and entering), and the two of them could have mini adventures. Matt was usually just the chauffeur and sidekick in these excursions; they were really all about Taryn. She'd known Matt for more than twenty years and he'd been humoring her for all of them, even when their first mode of transport had been nothing but their bikes and he'd ridden her around on the handlebars, her pigtails flying in the wind.

At first, she'd taken her 35 mm camera with them everywhere they went and snapped furiously at old barns, gnarled oak trees, and abandoned farmhouses with cracked windows and dilapidated roofs with daffodils growing through sagging porches. For every old house and ancient barn and warehouse they'd discovered, she created stories about the former inhabitants: who'd they been, what they'd seen, how they'd lived and worked. Matt had listened and humored her while her imagination spun tales from the past. She'd hated waiting almost a week for her pictures to be developed back then, but it was exciting, too. She'd had to be much more discriminate with her picture taking when developing the rolls cost money she didn't really have. She'd made sure every shot was framed to perfection. He'd had such patience with her as she got down on her knees, on her stomach, and even had him boost her up on his shoulders from time to time.

Then, on her fifteenth birthday, her grandmother gave her a Polaroid camera. That made things *really* interesting. Although the quality wasn't as good, she loved having the instantaneous product right in her hand. Sometimes, she took both cameras along with her and snapped until she'd run out of film.

She hadn't discovered her flair for painting until she was in high school. Her choices for an elective were between art and shop and even though she loved architecture, she was terrible at woodworking (her parents mistook her 4-H birdhouse for a sailboat), so art it was. Her teacher was tolerant and understanding and helped her to develop a skill she didn't even know she'd possessed.

The first building she had reconstructed in a painting was a barn. She loved barns, especially the ones that were used for tobacco because they had all the "little doors" as she'd called them when she was a kid. This particular barn was falling in, but still boasted brilliant red paint that shone in the sun and it also had a glorious cupola, something she almost never saw. Using her imagination and other barns of similar design for inspiration, she painted it as though it was in its former glory. The painting won her a prize at a regional art contest for high school students and the hobby of painting dilapidated buildings as they had once been took place.

When she was eighteen, she volunteered as a docent at a local historical home for the summer. During the eighteenth and nineteenth centuries, slave quarters existed on the grounds. Only half of one of the buildings still stood, although the sites of the others were marked. After gaining permission from the director, she spent a good part of her free time that summer reading through the letters, journals, and other documentation that were kept on hand at the museum from the family members and guests of the home during the time period. She also spent a lot of time at Vanderbilt University's research library. Within three months, she was able to create a painting of the grounds that included an eerily accurate representation of the mansion and all of the outbuildings, including the former slave quarters and a grist mill that was also in ruins. The painting still hung in the front hall of the museum. And it helped her eventually win a scholarship.

She wasn't entirely sure she believed Reagan's story about the dresser and the bedroom. She admitted there was something off about the house, but, *really*, a house that didn't want anybody to touch anything in it? Or rather—a room that didn't want anyone to touch anything in it? Not that she blamed the poor woman, of course. She didn't like her things bothered, either.

True, she felt something in the house. She wasn't going to deny that. And there was some kind of interesting sensation on the property she couldn't put her finger on. But she had felt that before. And, true, she wasn't sure she felt welcome there. But she had also felt that before. Of course, her vision *had* wavered in the living room. But maybe she could explain that, as well. She was tired, unfocused. It was hot outside, muggy. The air was old and musty. Who knew what kind of mold was inside those walls. She loved old buildings more than most people but black mold was serious business and could do funny things to people and it didn't take much of it to make you crazy.

There was always an explanation for the weird things that happened in old houses and she tried not to get too excited and jump to ghosts right away.

Besides, if anyone had a reason to want to believe in ghosts, it was her.

Dressed in cutoff jeans, an old Eagles T-shirt, and sneakers, Taryn headed back out to Windwood Farm in plenty of time to catch the evening light. She didn't bring her paints with her on this trip because she first liked to sketch what she would later put paintbrush to. She'd go over that sketch nearly a dozen times before she was happy with it. And frankly, she would never really be completely satisfied with it. She'd even go over it in her dreams. The photographs she took would help. She hadn't uploaded the previous ones to her laptop yet but she would that evening.

The weight of the day was starting to take its toll on her. She was still a little tired from the drive up. It had been three years since she'd worked at a private residence, even a deserted one, and the last one was a little bit of a disaster. The owner watched her like a hawk and made her a nervous wreck and she'd still been recovering from a difficult time in her life. The painting wasn't her best, even though her client, the Arts Council, was pleased with it. It was the longest month of her life.

Taryn spent the afternoon driving around town, checking out Vidalia's center and some of the local historical sites. There weren't many, but the town tried. They seemed to be particularly proud of their railroad and their depot was restored, offering visitors a small museum with relics from the Great Depression and mid-century that were especially interesting. Unfortunately, like many small towns in the south, urban sprawl paved the way for strip malls and big shoebox stores and Main Street was dead or on its way out. There had once been some charm to the town with its

37

turn-of-the-century courthouse and wide, tree-lined streets but much of that was lost when pitted against the heavy traffic flow, the vacant storefronts, and the flashing neon billboards.

She drove up on a ridge that overlooked the valley and was startled to see several housing developments full of identical structures, all with the same roofs and fences. They looked like dominoes from where she sat in her car. She'd heard from construction friends of hers that the new houses weren't built nearly as strong as the old ones, so she wouldn't be surprised if a strong push really would topple them over one by one.

Parking her car in the middle of the driveway, she hopped out and grabbed her canvas bag filled with her sketchpad and charcoals and started toward the middle of the wide, flat yard. The curtains fluttering in the breeze on the second floor caught her attention. Because she was looking up at the movement, she didn't notice the stone jutting out of the ground, and suddenly found herself on her face.

"Shit!" she screamed. Her ankle twisted painfully under her as her bag landed a few feet away. Turning over, she looked back at the culprit. A large creek stone was stuck in the ground behind her at an incredibly awkward angle, its sharp edge pointing up into the sky. "Good thing I didn't fall on it," she muttered to herself, imagining blood squirting from her head and not being discovered for days as she slowly bled to death from a head wound (she was nothing if not dramatic).

Crawling over to the rock, she inspected it more closely. There were several others around it, making a complete circle. On closer inspection it appeared to encircle a hole that had been filled in. She hoped whoever had done it had filled in well and with more than just loose dirt. She wasn't keen on the idea of falling into a century old abyss and left alone for several days…if she was ever discovered at all. She didn't do well with dark, hollow places.

"Hope it's not a sinkhole," she sighed. It wasn't unusual for her to talk to herself. She always worked alone and sometimes she got tired of the quietness. Recently, she actually tried working with an assistant once or twice and it made her nervous. Sometimes, though, she missed having noise. Talking inside her head made her feel crazy, but talking aloud made her feel eccentric in a nice kind of way.

Within a few minutes, she was able to quickly make a few sketches of the front of the house, including the maple and oak trees that filled the front yard and the winding driveway that wound its way back to the barns. She paid careful attention to the quivering curtains and boarded up door and windows and after finishing with the charcoal put her sketchpad away and pulled out her Nikon. "Okay, Miss Dixie. It's your turn. Do your thing."

The light was almost faded by then but she still had more than enough time to walk around the perimeter and do some sunset shots before getting back in the car and grabbing some dinner before going back to the hotel for the night. She would focus on one area of the house at a time as she painted but when she photographed, she liked to catch as many angles as possible.

It really *was* a beautiful area. Although she preferred the mountains to the east and even the flat, sultry thick deltas of the south, these manicured green valleys had their own gentle beauty that was hard to deny. She began to imagine what they must have looked like even half a century ago when the fields were full of tobacco and corn and the air was still and quiet.

She'd once been commissioned to paint an isolated cabin in West Virginia. It was located nearly twenty-five miles off the interstate. It was located so far off the main road that she'd ended up camping out up there the entire two weeks it took to get the job done. Amazed at how quiet the air had been without the sound of airplanes and cars around her, the stillness was both soothing and unsettling. She'd needed that at the time, even if she hadn't known it at the time. She didn't have cell phone service, television, or internet service the whole time she'd been up there, so she'd relied on her battery-powered CD player and the stack of CDs she'd brought with her. It was a bit like going through detox. By the time she was finished, she'd lost all track of what was going on in the rest of the world and she'd emerged as though she'd been living in a cocoon.

The "magic hour" wasn't so much an hour as it was a fleeting few minutes and she used every second to her advantage, snapping pictures left and right as she bent, stretched, and stooped, straining to get every angle of the house and property that was humanly possible (and then a few more). Her phone beeped furiously, a reminder she had missed her pre-planned phone call from Matt, but she ignored it. She couldn't call him back now. He would understand.

So used to framing the images she wanted, she barely took the time to even glance in the viewfinder before she moved on to the next image that caught her eye. She never checked her LCD screen while she was taking shots. She considered it bad luck. She and Miss Dixie shared a special rhythm and understood one another.

Taryn took the images that called to her. Every house and property spoke to her in a different way. Sometimes it was the yard. Sometimes it was a house's view. Sometimes it was a house's porch and the way it framed the world in front of it. There was no doubt about it, though. For Windwood Farm, it was the windows to the house that contained its soul. Even the ones that were boarded up and should have been emotionless called to her in ways that were inescapable. Without realizing it, she had soon taken hundreds of shots and nearly used up her memory card as the last rays of sunlight fell into the darkening sky.

Gathering up the remainder of her equipment, she tossed her canvas bag back into her car and turned around in the driveway. Again, she felt the unnerving feel of eyes on the back of her head as she deliberately drove down the gravel toward the gate. Her cell phone gave off its steady beat, the pale light flashing a radiant green into the car's dark interior. The faint smell of death clung to her clothes, prickling at her skin.


"**O**h, honey, we're just so glad you made it there okay!"

41

The woman on the other end of the line possessed the rough, whiskey-voiced sound older women tend to get after years of smoking. At first, Taryn thought she was talking to a man but then when the voice went into a coughing fit and Taryn heard the rattling sound in the back of her throat, she put it together.

"I made it here without any problems," Taryn agreed. "Found it just fine."

"Well, listen, I'm Priscilla and I'm the secretary for the Stokes County Historical Society. We've talked through email of course, but I thought you deserved a call now that you're here. I'm so sorry we weren't there to meet you but one of our members is in the hospital with pneumonia and we've all just been beside ourselves checking on her and taking care of her house. We've been running around like chickens with our heads cut off!" With that, the woman went into another coughing fit that concerned Taryn a great deal. She waited until she was finished before she spoke.

"That's okay. I'm fine. I went out there today and got started. It's a beautiful place," she added. Taryn was a little forlorn that her baked potato and soup were getting cold while she was having this conversation but she really couldn't put it off. The woman had already called her three times that day. She'd ignored those calls because she was busy. (Once she was driving, once she'd been in the bathtub, and the third time she'd been having a self-imposed time-out.)

"Oh yes, I knew you'd like it. It's a wonderful farm. Such a shame what's going to happen to it, isn't it? Of course, none of us remember what it used to look like, but you should have seen the farm on the other side of it, too. Now that was something to see! The house was one of the grandest in Kentucky. It was torn down years ago, though," Priscilla said sadly.

"Oh, what happened?" Taryn asked, both out of politeness and interest.

"A tornado took most of it and then it became dangerous. The family had the rest demolished and then they put in one of those subdivisions. It was a real southern beauty, though. The family, the Fitzgeralds, they owned most of the county at the time," Priscilla added.

"Wish I could have seen it," Taryn said sincerely.

"Well, listen, I'll let you get back to your dinner. I just wanted to let you know that we're grateful you're here and that we will see you soon!" As Priscilla hung up the phone, Taryn could hear her coughing again.

The coffee shop soup and baked potato were mostly warm by the time she got to them and the sweet tea felt nice after a long day out in the sun. She'd bought herself a pitcher and some packets at the store and was planning on making her own and taking it out to the farm with her while she worked. Her New Year's resolution included cutting down on caffeine. Normally, she tried not to unleash a decaffeinated version of herself on humanity, but she was really trying to get healthier these days.

"I wasn't even thinking when I called you earlier. It was just about dusk, wasn't it?" Matt apologized.

Taryn could hear him clanging on metal in the background. He was either cooking or thinking about cooking when she talked to him. They almost always put one another on speakerphone when they talked to each other. She wasn't offended. Neither one of them were capable of sitting still for long periods of time. They had to be doing something. She was currently in a partial stage of undressing herself and had her shirt over her head while she attempted to give him a muffled reply. "Hmuuhyphh..."

"Did you get anything accomplished today?"

Having tugged on her nightgown, she plugged in her flash drive and sat down in front of her computer in the middle of her hotel bed and began uploading her pictures. It was an old laptop and she wasn't optimistic that it was going to be a quick process. It never was. In the meantime, she fell back on the pillow and began flipping through the limited television channels.

"I think so. It's an interesting one. Lots of stone. Bad feelings, you know?"

"Already? That's fast. Hold on just a minute. I'm boiling over..."

Matt loved to cook more than he loved to do just about anything. As a physicist, cooking was his stress reliever, and it was a sad irony he didn't have anyone special in his life to share any of the grand meals he concocted. More often than not, he ended up tossing out all of the gourmet recipes he created night after night.

She did appreciate hearing about them, though. "So what are we having tonight?"

"Nothing special. Just some gumbo. I was feeling New Orleans. It's been stewing all day though. It smells so good. I also made some rosemary ciabatta to go with it. The whole house smells nice and toasty."

"Nice! I had Taco Bell for lunch. And to make it a little classier, I also stopped at Panera Bread and finished it off with a chocolate chip bagel."

Matt sighed. "You're going to die of food poisoning."

"Probably." She didn't tell him what she really had because she was afraid it would ruin her reputation.

A glance at the computer screen showed her the images were loading unreasonably slow this evening, although a few had already popped up. Oh well. There wasn't anything she could do to hurry them along.

"Do you want to hear about the house?" she asked. She knew he wouldn't ask on his own accord. Matt wouldn't think to. He was a little cerebral. Always trapped in his own head.

"Okay. But first, the bad feelings? Are they about the house or are they because..."

"I think it's the house, Matt. I don't think it's me this time," she answered shortly, a little annoyed.

"Are you sure?" he asked gently. "Because sometimes you can get the two confused. It's not easy working alone when you're in a place like that."

Trying to remember he was just being helpful, she closed her eyes and thought of all the times he had been supportive of her. "I know that sometimes I fall apart a little bit, but it's not like that. This is different. It's the house. Do you want to hear about it or not?"

"I do, I'm sorry. Go ahead."

"Okay...I can see why the Stokes County Historical Society is interested, even without the Governor part. The stonework is beautiful. The property is beautiful. I think the owner is doing a big disservice to someone. Instead of putting in a subdivision, if he doesn't want to renovate, then he could at least just build another house there and take advantage of that nice yard and those views. You're not going to get that with all those houses crammed in there."

Matt sighed. "Oooh! Did I mention that I got to give a tour of the lab today? We had visitors come down from DC! They were very impressed with..."

Taryn managed to tune him out after a few seconds. She (mostly) loved talking to Matt. He was her oldest friend and had stuck with her since childhood. He also understood her like few people did and his house provided refuge when she was feeling stressed and needed a break from the rest of the world, like she often did. There had even been a few times in the past when they tried to kindle a romance between them and sometimes it even worked, at least for small periods of time. But she could only handle him in small doses.

Between "The Golden Girls" on television and making the appropriate noises to Matt on the telephone to let him know she was indeed still listening to him speak, she almost forgot to check on her laptop and her pictures. She was just about to head to the small hotel-sized refrigerator to grab a drink when something caught her eye, and nearly made her topple onto the floor. "What the hell," she muttered, dropping the cell to the floor.

"Taryn?" came Matt's muffled response, sounding a mile away. "You okay?"

Grabbing the computer, she pulled it closer to her and began tapping some buttons, trying to make sense out of what she was seeing. Three, four, five, six...no, FIFTEEN of the eighteen photographs she'd taken of the downstairs rooms were unlike anything she had ever seen before.

When she'd taken them, the rooms were a little dark. They'd contained some furniture, but the furniture was dated, mismatched items from different time periods. Old calendars dotted some of the walls. Boxes lined the floors in two of the rooms. Stains were on the hardwood. The rooms had general unlived in feels to them. The windows were boarded up. The rooms were dark. They'd used flashlights to walk around and see.

But in her pictures...

The boards were gone. In their place were curtains; light, airy, lacy things that let in sunbeams that played across the floors. There was a settee in the parlor. Framed pictures were on the wall. There were no stains. There were no calendars on the walls.

The photographs were not focused. They weren't perfect. The lines were blurry and appeared to be superimposed atop the original ones, perhaps? But it was clear the rooms were the same, only they looked completely different. A glance through the rest of the pictures of the house showed her that none of them had come out. They were all black.

Picking the phone back up, she told an impatient Matt that she'd have to call him back. "Something came up," she explained in a whisper. "I'll tell you later."

For the next three hours, Taryn alternated between staring at her pictures, cleaning poor Miss Dixie, and poring over the internet. It wasn't really helpful. What she was supposed to type into Google, after all? Every time she tried to enter something into the search engine like "things in picture that aren't supposed to be there" the only thing she came up with were pages about camera defects. She was clearly in over her head as far as the paranormal pages went, too. She'd always been sensitive when it came to sappy commercials and cute babies and since Andrew's accident, she thought she picked up on some things that maybe other people didn't a little more often than not but wasn't this taking things just a little bit too far?

Still...a small part of her couldn't contain its excitement. She couldn't stop looking at the pictures. It was addictive! Once she got past the shock, she'd hooked up her printer and printed out two copies of every photo she'd taken and then got to work

48

painting them, just in case something happened to the prints themselves. What if she woke up in the morning and found the whole thing a dream? What if she'd accidentally taken too many anxiety pills and this was some sort of weird hallucination?

She wanted to remember what they looked like.

As she studied them now she appreciated the differences in the images. The rooms had a slight feminine feel to them that were oddly gentle against the darkness. They were clean and bright, but sadly lacking any personality. The rugs were bright, their colors cheerful, and care had been taken in choosing them since they matched but there weren't any knickknacks or flowers in vases. Just rooms, simple and tidy.

Sitting back, she smiled to herself as she put her paintbrushes away. It was dawn. She had been given a gift. After all these years, she'd finally been given something useful. She'd used her imagination and talent to try to help clients see the past. Now, for once, *she'd* actually been able to see it herself. It would probably never happen again, and it wasn't quite like going back in time, but it was a jolt she'd certainly never forget.

So the house was a little creepy and apparently bad enough to keep vandals out, but that didn't really concern her. She wasn't there to hurt it; she was there to make it come alive. She might not have believed in much when it came to the afterlife or religion, but she *did* believe in positive thinking. If she ignored the bad and focused on the good, then surely the house would work with her, right? Whatever was there had been dead and gone for a long, long time. And the past couldn't hurt her. At least, not *this* past. This wasn't her past, after all. This was someone else's past.

Then, why, suddenly, did she feel like crying?

She hadn't planned on sleeping past noon, but since she'd seen the sun come up, Taryn really didn't see a way around it. She needed more than just a few hours' worth of sleep if she was going to be able to function at all. Still, as she pulled herself into the small diner on the outskirts of town she felt jetlagged and disoriented. The young waitress looked at her sympathetically as she handed her a menu. "Can I get you something to drink?"

"Something with a lot of caffeine," she muttered. She'd start doing that tomorrow.

"I hear that," she laughed. She was tall and willowy and wore braces. Taryn estimated her to be anywhere from sixteen to twenty-five but the braces threw her off. "I'm having one of those days myself."

"You recommend anything?"

She shrugged. "We make everything, so it's all okay. Well, except for anything with fruit. That usually comes in a can unless it's summer, like now. I like the pancakes myself."

Handing her back the menu, Taryn nodded. "I'll take those then. And some sausage. And hey, are you from around here?"

"All my life, why?"

Taking a moment, Taryn described the house she was in town for. "Let me go put your order in and I'll be right back."

50

The restaurant was empty and she busied herself going through the pictures on her digital camera, still marveling at the images that shouldn't be there, until the waitress came back. Sliding into the seat across from her, she leaned into Taryn and started chatting. "You don't mind if I smoke, do you?"

"I didn't know anywhere still let you do that."

"Well, they don't," she said. "But nobody around here says anything or cares."

Taryn waited patiently while her waitress sat back and blew a few puffs, the white rings drifting off into the aisle and floating toward the empty counter. The sounds of dishes and silverware rattling back in the kitchen were the only noises in the otherwise quiet room. She must have missed the lunch crowd.

"I know the house, of course. Everyone does. It's kind of the town haunted house, if you know what I mean. Some people called it 'the Devil's house' growing up or just 'the stone gate to hell' because the gate out front is made of stone. Well, you know. We used to dare each other to go in there as kids. As teenagers, really. I'm Tammy, by the way."

"Taryn."

"Nice to meet you," she smiled, revealing her braces again. "Why you asking about the old place? You thinking of poking around in it?"

"Well, actually, I'm working there for a while," Taryn explained. "I've already poked." She took a few minutes and explained what she was doing and then laughed when Tammy shuddered.

51

"Better you than me, girlfriend, better you than me." When Tammy smiled, her face lit up and she possessed the kind of easygoing all-American beauty that Taryn envied. Even in her waitress uniform and braces, she managed to be pretty and perky. In contrast, Taryn still felt tired and haggard and her wrinkled khaki capris and buttoned-down western shirt (a size too big) made her feel dowdy.

"You ever go in there?" she asked, sensing a story waiting to be told.

"Once," Tammy answered conspiratorially. "But never any further than the kitchen. I was with my boyfriend at the time. We were sophomores. He'd just gotten his license, you know? Second day. It was the Friday after Thanksgiving and it was kind of cold like. There was a group of us and everyone else was poking around the property. Smoking, walking around. Just being kids, really. We decided to go *in* the house. Nobody else would. Lots of stories about that place, you know? Everyone daring everyone else to go in, but not too many people really did it. Anyway, we were going to be all brave and do it. So we walked up to the door, my boyfriend being all macho, and he pushed it in. We stepped inside and he pulled out the flashlight. He goes in first. It is **dead** quiet. Steps in, looks around. Says it's okay. I go in. He's all the way in the other room by the time I go inside. I'm halfway through the kitchen when he starts running back through the house and he's out the door. I have no idea why so I just stand there, kind of frozen like. Then I saw it. Well, first I heard it." Tammy shivered at the memory and snuffed out her cigarette into a saucer.

"What was it?" Without realizing it, Taryn leaned forward.

"A cry. It was the longest, saddest cry I'd ever heard in my life," Tammy whispered. "It came from upstairs. A woman. Well, a girl, really. Maybe my age. Like it was just breaking your heart. It shook the whole house. I felt it all the way down to my toes. I knew that cry. I've cried like that myself when my own heart was breaking. You know when you've had a breakup or felt like nobody loved you and your world was ending?" Tammy stopped talking and waited for Taryn to concede.

Not knowing quite how to answer, Taryn glanced down at the table and fiddled with her straw wrapper. "I know what you're talking about. Hey, I was a teenager once, right?" She said the last part hurriedly, hoping Tammy would continue. She did.

"I heard that and wanted to cry along with her. I couldn't move. But then I *did* move because right after that, this figure appeared in the kitchen door. It was solid black and it wanted me. Don't ask me how I knew—I just did. It was coming for me. It felt evil. You know what I mean? I turned and ran out of that house as fast as I could but I could feel it watching me all the way to the car. I will never forget it."

Tammy shivered again and rolled her eyes. "Sometimes, in my sleep, I still hear that cry. You know, the shadow, the evil thing? It bothered me, it scared me. But it was that cry, it was that sound that still bothers me. I'll never forget it as long as I live. I still don't know what my boyfriend saw. He won't talk about it."

She gazed absently out the window at the passing cars and Taryn studied her. She had no reason to doubt her story, especially

53

since it rang familiar. In fact, Taryn figured most people believed in the stories they told you, and there was a little grain of truth in everything.

The two women sat in companionable silence for a few moments, each one last in their own thoughts. A bell at the window rang and Tammy jumped up and brought Taryn's pancakes to her. "There are others in town that might be able to tell you their own stories. There has been stories about that place for years, ever since my mom was a little girl."

"Did anything happen there? I mean, is there a story? Did anyone die?"

"Not that I know of," Tammy replied. "I mean, not tragically or anything. Just old age and stuff like that. But I can talk to my grandma. She knows most of that stuff. Here, I'll give you my email." Hurriedly, Tammy jotted her information down on a slip of paper and then went back into the kitchen again.


Obviously, it wasn't the first time Taryn had heard a ghost story about the place she was painting. All old houses were meant to be haunted. It was almost an insult if they weren't. She had found that if there weren't any real tales to be told about the place, people were generally happy enough to make them up.

Tammy had seemed perfectly reliable and honest. But there were many reasons why a person might see or hear something in an old house. Taryn explained similar stories away for years. She had to. If she didn't, she might never step foot inside some of the places she worked in.

But she couldn't deny that Tammy's story had given her chills, similar to the ones she herself had felt inside the house. There was something going on inside and apparently more than one person had picked up on it. She needed to remember that. This house was different. She couldn't shrug these stories off like she had the others. Not after what she saw on her camera.

Once, on a job site in Georgia, she'd been painting a picture of an old plantation home. Most of it was no longer erect, but the local historical society received a grant to restore it. They had brought in Taryn, along with an architect, to create images of it.

Taryn didn't care for working with other people, but the architect was a young man her own age, just out of college, and he was friendly. He, too, preferred working on his own, so their paths didn't cross much and, when they did, it wasn't unpleasant. They'd both shared a love of history and the antebellum style of the home. Both were equally glad it was being restored.

Two weeks into the job, Taryn arrived onsite and found him standing outside, staring at the crumbling porch. He had a look on his face that was a cross between bemusement and horror. She touched his shoulder and he jumped into the air in shock.

"I'm sorry," he apologized. "I must have been thinking."

"Is everything okay?" she asked, feeling foolish because everything was obviously not okay.

He led her to a weeping willow tree and both sat down under it, the house in plain view in front of them. It was a beautiful structure with four large columns (signs of wealth) and a porch that had, at one time, stretched the length of the front. Even in its decay, she saw beauty in it and what it could be again one day.

"I crawled in through one of the back windows this morning," he said softly. "I know it's not safe, but well, you know..."

She nodded. Of course, she did it all the time. She had also done it here to this house, too.

"It was so quiet and peaceful. I walked around to the front of the house, real careful with my footing, and stayed where I knew the foundation was solid. There's a mantle in there that just blew my mind. Can't believe how perfect it is, considering that half the house is falling in."

Taryn let him talk without interruption, despite the fact that he kept taking long breaks in his speech.

"I wasn't inside for more than ten minutes, when I heard this sound. I wasn't sure what it was at first. It sounded like music. I thought maybe you were here and had your car radio on. I don't know. But something didn't feel right about it. Then, I realized it was coming from inside the house. And it wasn't a radio at all, but a piano."

The house was devoid of furnishings. There was no piano anywhere near it. They were at least five miles from the nearest inhabited house.

"Are you sure?" Taryn asked tentatively, but she knew he was certain of what he heard.

He nodded. "It went on for a few minutes and I just stood there and listened. It was maybe the most beautiful piano music I've ever heard. It felt as close as if I could just walk into the parlor and see someone sitting there, playing. And then it stopped. I thought it was over, but that's when the laughing started. A high, feminine laugh. A woman's for sure. It echoed through the rooms, like the sound was being soaked into the walls."

"What did you do?"

"I got out," he shrugged. "I couldn't do it."

Taryn knew he was confident in what he had heard. She knew he wasn't making the story up. She had spent many hours there in the house by herself and had felt like someone was watching her, listening to her talk to herself sometimes. But she'd never seen anything. She'd never heard anything. Sitting there under the tree with him, she almost felt disappointment.

She spent a productive day at the house, her experiences from her previous visits not repeated. She even tried walking around, taking more pictures, but they came out like any other picture she'd ever taken. *Maybe it's just my imagination*, she thought to herself. She probably *did* need more sleep.

The house felt quiet, at peace. In fact, the day was amazingly calm and still. It was a day straight out of a summer calendar: the birds were chirping, the butterflies flew about, the bees buzzed, and the clouds were fat and white against the bright blue sky. With her sandals kicked off and the grass curled up between her toes, Taryn was at a rare ease with herself. She listened to Bruce Robison and Tift Merritt while she worked, alternating their CDs and singing along when the spirit moved her.

The sketching went amazingly fast and within the first day she had most of the house outlined to her satisfaction. She enjoyed standing outside and working in this park-like setting and appreciated the fact that even though there were adjoining farms on either side of her (well, one was being developed as she worked) she rarely heard the sound of any kind of passing vehicle.

As she sketched, she thought about the house's former tenants. What had they been like? Had they thrown parties, celebrated a lot, worked hard? And what about the poor girl who had died? Taryn hoped she hadn't suffered much. The scent of decay and death were still overpowering at times, but she was starting to think that perhaps the house was picking up on some of the tragedies it had seen over the years: first Robert's wife and then his daughter.

Taryn also appreciated the fact that the Stokes County Historical Society had contracted her at all. She could use the money especially since she wasn't completely sure her car was going to hold up much longer. And the hotel wasn't bad either; at least, not as far as hotels went. The swimming pool was actually kind of nice and the free breakfast was more than just cereal and bananas. And then, of course, there was the added bonus of it having indoor corridors—*always* a sign she was staying in a swanky place.

But she wasn't sleeping well and she was tired. Taryn's dreams had bothered her over the past few nights; however, ever since she arrived in Vidalia (and what about that town name?). The previous night (morning) she dreamed she was falling into something dark and then awakened to the sound of crying. She was sure it had been someone else's cries at first, but since the dream had shaken her so much, she wasn't positive it hadn't been her own tears that woke her up.

And then there was the dream of being suffocated and unable to move. That was the worst one. It caused her to thrash about in her bed, as though held by ropes. She'd woken up struggling with her pillows and had slept with the TV on ever since. It might mean she was hearing used car commercials all night, but at least it offered her light and noise.

At the end of the day, after loading everything into the car, Taryn slipped her sandals back on and went for a walk around the property. With the boards off the door and windows, the house appeared more inviting. The stones were polished and reflected the late afternoon sunlight; the wide front porch easy to envision a swing and rocking chair on and full of guests enjoying the evening after a hard day's work. Taryn's appreciated talent might have been in showing the world what the past looked like, but her real talent was in imagining what the past held. Sometimes, it wasn't always welcomed. Sometimes it even hurt.

Staring at the contrast between the older part of the house and addition and holding her camera in her hands, Taryn felt the weight of the day on her shoulders. "Off to a good start," she whispered. "Going well." The house seemed to shimmer in the light, as if agreeing with her. A ripple of cool air sent chill bumps along her legs and up her arms. She continued walking, but crossed her arms over her chest.

Behind the house, the air was lighter and it was a little easier to breathe. It was also less magical somehow. She turned on her camera again and looked at the pictures she had taken that day. They were all normal images. But the ones before them, those, well, they were the special ones. *Yep*, she thought, *still there*. She hadn't dreamed them. *I'm not going crazy.*

It was during this time of the day that she should be winding down and feeling good about what she had done, but it was usually by now when she felt the loneliest. She wasn't due to talk to Matt tonight, although she knew she could call him and probably should, especially after what happened. The sinking feeling in the pit of her stomach that had plagued her for months and months was getting better there for a while, but she imagined she would always suffer setbacks.

When the last rays of light had fallen behind the barn, she made her way back to her car and got in. She didn't know why people were so afraid of the house; it just seemed sad to her.

# Chapter 4

It had been all she could do not to hop in her car and drive back to the house in the middle of the night to take more pictures when she first saw them on her computer screen. She was giddy at the thought of capturing more images and being transported back into the past—creepy shadow guy that Tammy talked about not included. Miss Dixie, who had always been one of her prized (if not the most prized) possessions now took a place of honor in her hotel room. She set her next to her second favorite object, the television, so that she could keep an eye on both equally.

Once she calmed down, she paced back and forth across the hotel room's multi-colored carpeted floor and had a good long talk with herself. What if this was a one-time thing? What if it was just going to happen at certain times? Should she get back out there right away and take more pictures? And what time period were the pictures from? Well, that question was easy enough to answer. They had to be from the 1920s or 30s. Nobody had really lived in the house after that and the furnishings hadn't looked 19th century. But why that time period and not anything before or after?

On a lark, she tried taking pictures of her hotel room, wondering if anything would show up that wasn't supposed to be there, but they came back normal: just her messy clothes rack, cluttered sink, and shoes kicked off all over the floor. That had been disappointing, but she figured it was probably better than them showing some of the other things that had probably gone on in the room before her stay (things she definitely didn't want to think about if she was going to sleep on the bed).

In disappointment, she thought back to some of the other places she'd worked in the past, like the old farmhouse in Vermont with its gables and wrap-around porch. It was missing the entire backside and hadn't been lived in for almost fifty years. It was so homey, though, and inviting. She'd loved to see what it looked like in its prime. It was too bad her camera hadn't picked up anything there. Or the house in Mississippi. If only the camera could have picked up on something there and Andrew could have seen the piano making the beautiful music...He'd never had that experience again after that particular house, no matter how many jobs he'd worked on as historical architect.

But she couldn't think about Andrew right now or the other jobs they'd worked on together after Mississippi.

Taryn had spent her entire professional career showing her clients the past and helping them see, but this was the first time she'd ever been able to see for herself. Nobody had ever given that experience to her.

She did briefly wonder if she should contact Reagan or the members of the Stokes County Historical Society and show them what she had, but this wasn't a thought she entertained for very long. They'd either think she was crazy or, more likely, they'd be over there harassing her about it every day. No, she wanted to keep this to herself as long as possible. She didn't like a crowd.

What she wanted was to take more pictures and see more stuff! What she wanted was to run around to every old building she could find and snap images like crazy, hoping to see things from the past emerge.

But she was afraid.

Since returning to the house, she tried capturing more images and they'd all come back normal. That had been a huge letdown for her. She hadn't heard or seen anything unusual either, despite Tammy's stories about the house being haunted and her previous experiences. That was also disappointing. She didn't want to see a ghost, if there were such things, but to be completely cut off like that once the door opened for her a little bit made her feel like she had done something wrong.

She appreciated the house and was even starting to love it, so she didn't understand why it wasn't revealing itself to her, or whatever you wanted to call it. If it was supposed to be so haunted, then why hadn't she heard anything or seen anything? Why hadn't Miss Dixie picked up on anything more? She'd been back inside almost every day since working there for the past week and a half. Once, and she was even a little embarrassed to admit it, she had even stood at the bottom of the stairs, and called out to the "ghosts" and given them "permission" to reveal themselves.

Nothing. Not even a "boo."

Of course, she was a little concerned about her sanity but that wasn't unusual. There were several counselors, a psychiatrist, an ex-boyfriend, and a family doctor who would say the same thing.

If it weren't for the fact that she still had the feeling there was something unsettling about the farm and, of course, the pictures themselves then she might have just chalked the whole thing up to some mass hallucination and urban legend. Or something.

Settling into a routine was easy for Taryn, despite the excitement of the first few days on the farm. She generally tried to wake up a little bit before dawn so that she could shower, eat a quick breakfast of cold cereal and toast, stop somewhere along the way to grab a cola (she'd start cutting back the next day, she told herself each morning), and then have her easel and paints set up and ready by the time the sun broke through the sky.

It was still cool in the early summer morning air and the fog enveloped the house, cutting out the world around it. The river was only a few miles away and since the farm was located high on a ridge, the thick mist rose from the valleys to meet the barns and edge of the yard like billowing curtains. As it dissipated late into the morning, she could start making out the subdivisions and signs of town, and that was always a little disheartening. For at least an hour or two, she was able to pretend she was trapped in time, alone in the mid-20th century, with the rest of the world blocked out.

When she first set out, the air was chilly and she'd slip on a cardigan or sweatshirt. By afternoon, though, with the sun high in the sky, it would be humid and sticky and she'd peel off her outer layer and toss it on the ground. Then she'd continue painting in her tank top and cut off shorts with her reddish blonde hair slicked back in a ponytail. Sometimes she even started out with it wet; fresh out of the shower. She never saw anyone out there, not after the first day when Reagan showed her around.

At around 3:00 pm, she'd stop for the day and load everything back into the car. Sometimes she'd head back to the hotel and grab a nap, and other times she'd find a place to eat first, depending on how hungry she was. She almost always snacked throughout the day on bananas, sandwiches she'd made before she left the hotel, and candy bars she kept in her cooler. She'd never been a huge eater and rarely ate more than one big meal a day, so she let her stomach guide her.

She wasn't finished working once she arrived back at her hotel. Although she put her paints up, she had other work to tend to. Taryn was basically a one-woman show and ran a small business that kept her on her toes. Keeping up with her correspondence was important. She was never entirely sure how the people who found her did, but they always seemed to locate her for her services. There were emails from all over the country, from historical societies to museums and private individuals, asking for her work. How much did she charge? How much of an existing structure did she need in order to recreate the entire thing as it once was? These were easy questions to answer, for the most part. She replied and asked for pictures, if they had any.

To others she answered, regretfully, that no, she could not work pro bono, not at this time. She was not a nonprofit organization. She must eat just like everyone else. Her car also required insurance and there was rent to pay, despite the fact she was hardly ever there.

In an interview with a regional travel magazine last year, the interviewer asked her how she chose her assignments. Surely, location had something to do with it. And, of course, location did. She loved to travel and going to destinations she'd never been to before (like the crumbling antebellum mansion in Mississippi or the amazing scenery in Montana) had definitely had its perks. Sometimes, too, she liked to stay close to home, so she often took jobs based near her home base of Nashville. But more often than not, she listened to the ones that called to her. That's really why she requested the pictures. In college, when she was studying Historic Preservation at Middle Tennessee State University in Murfreesboro, even before she began her internship and started her hands-on experience at Belmont Mansion in Nashville, the images of some places called to her before others did. She had more than just an eye for some things—she had an *ear* for them.

Taryn was always keeping her eyes and ears out for the next place. Her feet itched for the next adventure and she didn't like grass to grow under her feet. Not for long. Her bank account wouldn't let it, for one, and although she liked to pop back into Nashville to check on her apartment and make sure everything was still there, she preferred to spend as little time as possible in the cramped quarters. On the road, she had space; freedom to move around. In Nashville, she rented a studio apartment with a kitchenette and a range with one and a half burners that actually worked and a microwave with a short in it and an elevator that smelled like melting cheese.

She'd owned a house once, with log cabin furniture and handmade quilts and knickknacks that had been picked up at antique stores all over the country and lovingly carted back home with excitement. Those were all in a storage unit and had been locked up for years. She wasn't sure she could ever look at any of those again.

Answering her correspondence took up a lot of her time. Catching up with her television shows and reading took up the rest. Her parents, before the plane crash in her teens, taught her that you could never have too many books going at once. She learned the same went with television shows. Taryn didn't believe in just watching one show, she watched them all. An ex-boyfriend compared watching TV with her to watching a tennis match with a sea otter on speed. She never stayed with anything for very long, but she could follow everything very well. She easily switched from a comedy, a talk show, a murder mystery, and an infomercial within a matter of seconds and instantly know what was going on within all of them with little to no difficulty. It was a skill she proudly developed over time.

She could do the same with books.

Her parents hadn't been book snobs, and neither was she. This was something that embarrassed Matt to no end. "How can you possibly read that?" he'd mutter with disgust as she'd gleefully delve into a trashy bodice-ripper without any apologies.

"The same way you can read *that*," she'd point to the leather-bound copy of whatever pretentious classic he was holding. "I tried to read it at least a dozen times and I couldn't figure out what the hell was going on."

"It's-," he'd start to object.

"I know who it is," she would roll her eyes. "But that's the problem with literature. So much of it seems to be so esoteric. It's like it has to be weird for people to think it's any good. I think it's kind of like the emperor's new clothes and I'm just the one in the middle of the room telling everyone that he's actually naked."

Of course, she did like a lot of the classics, but she also liked to mix things up and read a little bit of everything. Mostly, she liked to get Matt's goat now and then and keep him on his toes. And he knew that. He'd slip her some Dickens to keep her honest and she'd read him VC Andrews to add some trash to his life and they were able to even out one another in that way. It kept their friendship fresh.

The routine kept the days going as quickly and smoothly as possible, but there still wasn't a whole lot she could do about the nights. They were a problem. Taryn always had problems with nights. She'd prowled as a child, something her parents were concerned enough about to take her to the doctor for over and over again growing up. A team of medical experts had diagnosed her with everything from sleep paralysis to nightmares and insomnia and later the ambiguous "night terrors." Some nights she couldn't sleep at all. She'd lay there and toss and turn and stare at the ceiling, a million thoughts running through her head at once, scrambled through her head like a remote control stuck flipping through all of the channels at high speed. When she'd explained this to one psychiatrist he'd decided she'd had ADD (no ADHD when she was a child) and she'd been put on medication. That made it worse. Some nights she went into an instant sleep and had nightmares so terrible she woke up screaming, grasping at the sheets in anguish and then wouldn't sleep for days, terrified at the thought of closing her eyes. She wouldn't dare tell anyone of the images she saw when she closed her eyes. The only one she came close to confiding in was her grandmother on her mother's side; someone who also has somewhat of an inkling of what she was going through.

When Taryn was eight, her grandmother pulled her up into her fluffy featherbed on a hot summer night and comforted her into her saggy armpits (that always smelled like baby powder) and whispered words into her ears she couldn't quite remember these years later but, at the time, were comforting. Taryn had drifted off to sleep in the scent that was a little musty and a little sweet and had slept the first dreamless night she'd had in almost a year. She was only supposed to be there for a weekend, but her parents let her stay for a week and later, for a month. Probably relieved to be away from the drama, they ended up letting her stay there for her fourth grade year and enrolled her in school in the small town of Franklin, Tennessee, convincing themselves it was probably better for her to be out of the big city of Nashville anyway and since they were both out of town so much for research, Taryn ended up spending the rest of her childhood with her grandmother until she passed away eight years later, only a year after Taryn's parents.

Nobody, not her friends and especially not her boyfriends, knew Taryn continued to sleep with her grandmother until the day she passed away and that, in fact, Taryn had been in bed with her at her time of death.

As an adult, she still found it difficult to sleep alone.

Taryn was tired when she showed up at the house early the next morning. She stayed up the night before watching some show on the Lifetime Movie Network about a woman who sued another woman for stealing her husband. Taryn wasn't completely sure why the women were fighting over the man in question, he didn't seem like that much of a prize, but at two o'clock in the morning, it had seemed like a fine idea to stay up and watch it, and now she was paying for it. When she was this tired it was hard to focus and the world felt off-kilter, just a little bit more unreal.

It rained sometime during the night and the grass was still wet. Her boots were sticking in the ground and clumps of mud stuck to the bottoms with every step she took. She was glad she'd ditched her usual summer sandals and was wearing something more practical.

The house looked even more ominous in this light, set against the gray sky, but there were peaks of sunlight trying to squirm through the clouds and there were prickles of heat against her skin telling her it would still be a hot day if given the chance. It would burn off the fog soon enough. Such was Kentucky.

Within a few minutes, she had set up her easel and paints and started working on the masonry, the hardest part of the house. Since part of the house had fallen down so many years ago, it was hard to imagine what it might have looked like, but the stones were still there and it wasn't difficult to see their colors and textures. They still shimmered, even in the dense fog and strained light of the early morning mist. Where some people might have seen dark grays and somber tones, she saw jewels and coppers. Each stone had its own personality and she painted each one so that it told its story through her brush. It was a shame, really, that the wing had collapsed, but it had done so in such a beautiful jumbled mess. She was considering doing an entirely separate painting of it just because it had landed so deliciously intricately, almost like a sculpture or Roman ruins. There were people who lived in mansions who would pay to have such structures intentionally built in front of their houses today in their gardens. She hoped someone would make use of the stones and come and cart them away and they wouldn't end up in the landfill. Since Reagan was a contractor, she figured he would do something with them or at the very least donate them to the Habitat for Humanity Restore. Most of them were still in very good condition and probably of some historical value.

After several hours of what she thought was pretty good work on her part, she stepped back and admired her own work, gave herself a pat on the back, and took a break. "Well done, old girl," she said aloud and then *literally* gave herself a pat on the back because, after all, she believed if you didn't do it, then nobody else would.

The sun had come out by then and the ground was starting to dry, but it was still very muddy so she headed to the car and sat on the hood while she ate her lunch—leftover Subway from the night before.

Reagan had taken the boards off the windows like she had asked, and now that the sun had risen in the sky it caught the upstairs window and the glare made it appear to wink at her. In fact, it seemed to look right at her. Shielding her eyes, she turned away. "Damn it," she muttered, as she looked at the ground and took another bite. The glare was so bright, however; she couldn't ignore it.

She had grown used to the uneasy feeling she'd developed on the first day and thought she might be making friends with the house. It didn't feel as unwelcoming to her as it did in the beginning and she was almost certain it had even preened a little today while she was painting it, as though it knew it was posing for something that would make it immortal.

Taryn was not a religious person, and wasn't even sure she believed in God, or one powerful entity at all, but she did believe in energy and nature and if there was something bigger than herself in the universe, she always felt it outside when she was alone. She never found it inside the walls of a church or listening to someone preach. Sometimes, while she was painting, she'd get so lost in thought and deep into her picture that she even thought she might becoming a part of it, or with the world around her. It was the closest thing she'd ever had to a religious experience and the feeling of euphoria it gave her was similar to the one she'd gotten off some pain pills when she'd had her wisdom teeth removed.

All of a sudden, a loud crash from inside the house sang out and caused her to jump off the hood and drop her sandwich to the ground. "So much for the five-second rule," she cursed as she watched it immediately get covered with mud and ants. She was hungry, but not *that* hungry.

Still, she was curious about the noise. She didn't think anyone was in the house and it had been a couple of days since she'd been inside. "Eh, why not?" she mumbled, and made her way to the front door. "What's it going to do?"

Taken a little aback by the amount of darkness that existed even with the windows uncovered, it took her a moment to adjust her eyes when she stepped inside. The living room was cleared of any items and was stark and empty. Taryn thought this made it feel less intimidating than before; the boxes had made it feel more lived in, like someone was coming back. Even the curtains were gone. The peeling wallpaper was still there, though, and it gently flapped as she walked by, stirred by her movements– the only testament to the fact she was actually there.

The hardwood floors were rock-solid and didn't make a sound as she moved through the rooms. Not a squeak was made. She was surprised by the lack of dust and smiled at the fact that Mrs. Jones had dusted them; that effort was made to sweep the house before it was demolished. It must be a southern thing to clean something before killing it– to fix something before destroying it. She marveled at the beautiful fireplace mantle, so detailed and ornate and yet at the staircase banister, so simple and plain. There seemed to be no rhyme or reason as to why money was spent on some fixtures and not on others. Clearly, the original owners had possessed money, yet had been selective about how it was spent.

The dining room and kitchen were also bare of belongings, as were the downstairs closets. There obviously wasn't anything downstairs that could have made a noise so loud she was able to hear it from outside. At any rate, it was as quiet as a church now, or a library. It was hard to imagine this place ever filled with the sounds of a family: laughter, singing, dancing, chattering...Yet the house must have possessed such things and been host to such activities at one time, right? Someone lived in the house and loved it once. Yet there were no echoes of this former life in it now. She could barely even hear own breathing.

Without the boards on the windows and door, it was slightly easier to see. She thought (hoped) the extra light might make the house feel more gracious, yet the welcoming feeling she'd experienced outside disappeared as soon as she stepped through the front door.

Once she circled through the downstairs, she made her way to the first set of stairs in the living room. As soon as she put her foot on the first step, a roar so loud she felt as though her eardrums would pop from the deafening sound filled the room to a raucous level. Staggering, she fell backward and scraped her skin against the wooden stairs behind her. As she clutched at her chest, she pushed against an invisible force that seemed to thrust against her, holding her down. The rumble continued all around her, filling the air at an incredible volume, the sound neither man nor animal.

An astonishing wind swept through the room and up the staircase, whipping her hair and sending hot air down her throat, making her unable to talk or scream. Gasping for breath, she struggled for breath and began choking, gagging, wheezing. The front door closed with a bang, shaking the walls. In horror, she watched small, thin cracks climb the living room windows and then gasped as the glass shattered and flew out into the yard in hundreds of pieces. Using her hands and sheer strength, Taryn managed to grab onto the banister and pull her way up, inch by inch. Finally, by wrapping her legs around it, she was able to straddle it. Turning her back to the door and wind, she caught her breath. Using what energy she had left, she screamed with everything she had, "WHAT DO YOU WANT!?"

As quickly as it started, everything stopped.

Taryn was left on the banister, a little kid who had simply been caught sliding down from the top of the stairs. There was utter stillness again with no sign that anything had happened, other than the fact that the windows were broken and the door was closed.

Shaken, she unwound herself from the banister and ran out the front door, not bothering to close it behind her. She'd let the ghost deal with that.

# Chapter 5

She let 24 hours pass by before she picked up the phone and called Matt. Oddly enough—or maybe not—Reagan had not been too surprised when she called him. "Those windows are so old, I'm surprised they lasted this long," he muttered. "Well, it will be a mess to clean up. Just be careful in the grass!" She wondered how he would react when he saw just how many pieces they had actually shattered into.

She knew she should have called Matt sooner. She also knew he would already know something was wrong because he was intuitive that way; still, he knew better than to press. He was the only person in her life that knew Taryn as well as her grandmother did, but he'd learned a long time ago that it was better to let Taryn come to him first. The one time he had pushed, he'd pushed too hard and he nearly lost her. After that, she didn't speak to him for almost four years.

"Hey you," he spoke lightly, but she thought she heard his voice tense up. "You holding up okay up there?"

"Just barely," she answered. "Something's really wrong, Matt. Something bad."

"Tell me."

So she did. This time, she started at the beginning and told him everything she'd felt, seen, and thought about Windwood Farm. She didn't leave anything out, including what the waitress had told her. When she was finished, she asked him what he thought.

Matt, of course, had a very analytical mind and thought everything through with precision. That didn't mean he wasn't extremely open-minded. He might be a scientist, but he was also a spiritualist and it was something she loved about him. He lived on both sides of the line.

"There's something dark in the house, Taryn, and I don't think you're being careful enough about it. You shouldn't go back in there and if you do, you need to protect yourself. Are you using sage?"

It was nearly impossible not to smile. After all, he might work for NASA, but still wore a pentagram around his neck. He studied aerospace engineering, but occasionally wrote blog entries for one of the most popular Wiccan blogs on the internet. He knew his stuff.

"I don't have any on me, no."

"I could send you some if you'd like. Or you could drive to Lexington. There's a shop there. I can send you the directions. I have a friend who could go ahead and have some ready for you at the counter. It's very simple."

That was Matt. He was always ready to take care of her. He was nothing if not practical.

"It scared me. Not in the 'the ghost wants me soul' sense, but in the 'it could kill me' sense. It felt physical, Matt. I didn't think spirits could be like that. When I talked to it, it stopped. Do you think that's the key? That by communicating with it, I could make it stop?"

"I can't tell you what it is. It might be a ghost, it might be leftover energy. It might just be a hologram of sorts. Until you know what you're dealing with, my advice is to just stay away from it. Don't put yourself in its path. Your energy might feed it, give it more energy. The fact the house is going to be demolished, the change it's feeling, that might be feeding it as well. Finish your painting and leave. You don't know what's going on there. Please, Taryn. I have a bad feeling about this and I'm rarely wrong where you're concerned."

"Why me, though, Matt? I've worked in plenty of old houses before. Not to mention all the ones we used to break into. Why now?" That was her biggest question, really. Why had this started all at once? It must *mean* something, right?

"I don't know," he answered wearily. "Maybe it senses something in you. Maybe you're sensitive in a way that it connects with. I'm not saying you're weak—don't get me wrong on this—but maybe with what happened, there's something going on that it can connect with. This is why you need to be careful."

"And I thought it was just because the house knew how much I respected it."

When she hung up the phone, she felt even more confused than before. She did, however, feel better having talked to someone else about it. She'd never been able to talk to her parents the way she'd been able to talk to her grandmother or Matt. Losing her parents made her sad, in the way losing a favorite aunt or uncle or anyone else she'd gotten used to would make her sad. But she hadn't felt any real grief. She'd barely known them. Losing her

79

grandmother had felt like losing her soul mate. And then Andrew...like losing a limb. But Matt knew her and understood her. She felt better having voiced her fears and knowing she wasn't crazy. That helped.

The hotel didn't have a gym, but that was okay. She wasn't big on exercises that felt like exercising. Her body completely rebelled if she tried to make it do anything to gain muscle or lose weight. She did like swimming, however, and the hotel boasted both an indoor and outdoor pool, as well as a hot tub.

After taking several laps in the pool, she slid into the hot tub and turned on the jets, letting them beat against her back. She turned her nose up at the sign warning her not to swim alone (what about business people? What were they supposed to do?) and tried to relax. The day's events had shaken her up and taken off some of the excitement of the pictures. She obviously couldn't deny there was something in the house, but she still wasn't convinced that it was a ghost. At least, now that she was away from the house she wasn't convinced it was a ghost. When she was inside the house, she was certain it was. But she wasn't being rationale then. Whatever it was, though, it didn't seem to want her there. Or anybody for that matter, considering the shape of the house itself and the fact everyone more or less left it alone.

Matt was worried about her and that was normal. He'd been trying to take care of her since she was a little kid. Once, when she was in college, he even called her dorm director when she had the flu and made sure she was keeping fluids down and taking her anti-nausea medication. The other girls in the dorm swooned over him whenever he came to visit and went on and on about how much of a gentleman he was because he held the door open for her, took her out to dinner to nice places, and dressed well. All of those things she appreciated as well, and he really *was* a good friend, but his concern was sometimes stifling. She tried not to overburden him with too many problems because he wanted to take them on as his own and at times stressed about them more than she did.

The water felt hot and secure and flowed over her like a blanket. In this large room with the classical Muzak playing and the sky turning dusky and pink, it was easy to forget about the cold, dark rooms of Windwood Farm and whatever lurked in them.

She almost didn't notice when the door opened and someone else entered the pool area. The sound was far away, in another time, and although she was aware that someone else invaded her space, she didn't give it much thought until the water moved abruptly and splashed against her face—a sign that someone else had entered the water.

The man was pale and paunchy and probably in his early forties. He had dark hair that was still thick and curly and maybe twenty pounds lighter and ten years earlier, he would have been attractive. "Hello," he said cheerfully. She thought she detected a slight northern accent.

"Hi," she smiled quickly and then closed her eyes; friendly but not encouraging.

A few seconds passed and she thought she might actually be able to relax a little longer in peace and quiet before the stranger started talking again. "You in town for business?"

Wishing she'd brought her book with her, she opened her eyes and peered at him. He was staying a respectable distance away from her on the other side of the hot tub, but taking a bath with a stranger was always a little uncomfortable. There were security cameras up, though, and the front desk was visible from where she sat. She wasn't nervous, just irritated. "Yes, I'm here working."

"Me too," he offered. "Pharmaceutical rep. I come through here about every three months. What are you in for?"

"I'm an artist," she replied simply and hoped he would leave it at that, and get the hint that she was not in the mood for conversation.

"Oh, that's interesting. So you're a painter?"

"Multi-media, actually, but I am here for a painting," she explained with a sigh. He wasn't going to let her off that easily. He seemed harmless, but she just wasn't in the mood for small talk. This happened almost every place she traveled to and even though it never amounted to much more than an annoyance, there were times when she wished she had a companion or at least a wedding ring to throw them off. It was never young, good-looking men who tried to talk to her, either, or else she might have felt differently. In fact, this guy was younger than most. The last one who tried to pick her up was literally old enough to be her grandpa.

"So does that actually pay money?" he asked with genuine interest, moving a little closer.

"No, I mostly get paid in geese these days, but the eggs are good on the black market," she replied.

He looked a little taken aback at first and then decided to laugh. "I'm sorry. I don't know why I asked that. I'm not even allowed to talk about the kind of money I make," he confided, then leaned a little closer to her. "But you wouldn't believe it, really. Almost six figures last year."

"Wow," she said drily. "That's great."

"Yeah," he nodded enthusiastically. "If more people knew that then everyone would be trying to become one. It's all in you know, though."

"Hmmm."

Before he decided to share any other pertinent information, she figured she ought to make her move. "Well, good luck with your business. I've got to get back to my room."

As she rose up out of the water, she was painfully aware of her small bathing suit and the way it was riding up her backside. If she tried to fix it, though, it would draw attention straight to it and she didn't want him ogling her any more than he already was. His eyes bored into her chest as they said goodbye.

"Well, listen, I'm going out for dinner tonight and if you'd like to join me—" he started.

"I'm sorry," she cut him off with what she hoped sounded like genuine regret. "But I've got other plans. I'm sure I'll see you later."

Grabbing her towel and room key, she sailed out the door and scooted on down the corridor to her room, thankful she didn't have far to go.

He was probably harmless and dinner might have even been fun on some levels, but she just couldn't do it. She had made friends on the road before and it always ended a little sadly for her since the friendship never lasted. She would move on or he would move on and that was the end of that. Lack of permanency depressed her, so she tried to avoid situations that reminded her of that fact every chance she got.

Feeling lighter in step after a good night's sleep, Taryn packed her bags for the morning and drove to the diner for breakfast. She was happy to see Tammy working when she walked through the door and she threw up her hand in a quick wave. Tammy smiled and pointed to her section and Taryn nodded in agreement and slid into a booth.

"I talked to Granny," Tammy whispered when she brought the laminated menu over to her, looking over her shoulder at the manager behind the counter. "You know, about the house? She said she remembered a few things about it that might be helpful. A few things that you might want to know."

"Yeah, well, I could use anything you could throw my way, that's for sure," Taryn muttered.

Tammy looked at her sympathetically. "You've been seeing things, haven't you?" she asked.

Taryn nodded. "You could say that. Hearing them and feeling them, more accurately." She wasn't ready to talk to anyone else about the photographs yet. They felt too personal.

"My granny said you might. Some people are more sensitive than others, that's what she says. But the house and what haunts it? It's because of the old man that lived there, the one from a long time ago, back from when she was a little girl. He was awful, she said. Nobody much cared for him. I don't know what he was meant to have done but nobody did a whole lot of grieving when he died if you know what I mean. She said that everybody said that when he finally kicked the bucket, most folks thought it was just as much from meanness as it was from a heart attack or whatever. She thinks it's his ghost that haunts the place and that's why the place is so mad, because he was always so mad. So she told me to tell you to be careful, to stay away if you can help it. He was never any good. And that even in death, he's probably pretty awful."

"Yeah, well, I've got a lot of work to do yet. Unfortunately, I can't stay away. But I appreciate your help," Taryn said warmly, honestly grateful for any information she was able to gather at this point.

After she'd eaten her short stack of pancakes and sausage and finished off two glasses of apple juice, she was leaving a couple

85

of dollars under the plate when Tammy poked her head back from around the kitchen door again, a stack of dirty dishes in her hand. "Hey, I forgot something I was supposed to tell you!"

"What was that?"

"It might not be important, but it was about his daughter. She died real young, eighteen I think, but nobody knows how. Some kind of weird illness, but he wouldn't talk about it. Didn't look like murder or anything, you know, checked out with the coroner, but folks were suspicious. They talked about it for a long time. Just thought you should know," she shrugged, and then disappeared again.

Taryn thought about this on the long drive back to Windwood Farm.


Of course, she knew he'd had a daughter. Reagan had mentioned it on the first day and she'd been in the bedroom and had seen her things. In fact, her bedroom had been left a virtual shrine, unlike the other rooms which were all but cleared out of everything. She'd never seen anything like it before. It hadn't escaped her attention that nearly every corner of the house was void of articles of the past except the daughter's room which was horror movie intact with relics that should have been looted by vandals more than fifty years ago. And perhaps some of it had been carried off a little at a time. She had no idea how much of it was really left since there was nothing to compare it to. But the fact remained that a lot of it really did still linger...Why? Was there really a thin veil covering that room that separated it from the rest of the house? A veil that kept anyone from disturbing it?

The afternoon went by without a hitch, but she felt uncomfortable, watched. She was unable to get into the painting like she usually did and even the quietness around her, which she usually found peaceful and even a little cathartic, bothered her. It felt pressing, probing, and not quite right. The batteries in her CD player died in the middle of her favorite Allison Moorer CD and that made her mad and threw her off just as she was working on the maple leaves. She ended up turning on her car radio and risked running her battery down just so she could listen to some music. The background noise helped and made her feel less alone, although what passed as "country" music today left a bad taste in her mouth and sounded more like what she listened to in the 80s on the pop stations.

On a lark, to get out of her funk, she tried walking around the house, taking pictures of the exterior, and frequently (excitedly) checking her LCD screen. The pictures came out looking ordinary, however, without any furniture or figures showing up who shouldn't be there. She couldn't help but feel disappointed. Had it just been a fluke? A one-time thing? Maybe it *was* just a flaw in her camera after all...She really was completely alone. Not that she wanted a repeat of what had happened on the staircase, but it was a little upsetting that not even the ghosts wanted to communicate with her. *Maybe I shouldn't have shouted at it*, she thought. *Then again, it did break windows at me and try to suffocate me?* Maybe she was wrong in thinking that they weren't ghosts. Maybe everyone else in town was right.

Nothing happened that day, nothing she could really vocalize or tell anyone about, but there was a moment when she turned her back to the house to load up her car and the tiny hairs on the back of her neck stood up at attention. She could have sworn someone was watching her and as she packed away the last of her equipment she felt the air give around her, almost as if the house itself was breathing a sigh of relief.

She was torn between feeling relieved and feeling disappointed when she left. Part of her was terrified at what was going on. When she'd been inside the house, she'd been petrified; afraid. Listening to Tammy talk, she questioned her own sanity about even returning to the farm day after day to work out there alone. Like any sane person, she didn't want to be accosted by an evil spirit or awful dead guy who been buried for more than seventy-five years. So that part of her was relieved that nothing else was happening.

But the other part of her was disappointed. That part actually wanted to see a little more. That part was almost proud that, for whatever reason, she'd been chosen (or whatever) to see the images in the photographs. That part of her felt a connection with the home and the farm and wanted to learn more about what was going on. That part of her thought that maybe, if she could see a little more, then perhaps there was hope that her own past could be brought back to life.

Feeling foolish, she pushed on the accelerator a little harder than she needed to as she sped out of the drive. In the rearview mirror the house looked sad, abandoned, neglected. It didn't look haunted by an evil spirit or negative forces. But Taryn knew, without a doubt, that there was something at unrest within the walls and on the grounds and this was one job that wouldn't be easy to leave behind.

The town of Vidalia, (she'd never get used to saying that name without smiling) was a small one that had tried unsuccessfully to grow into something it wasn't. There were a few pretty historical buildings on Main Street, however, and it was a picturesque place with its green hills and valleys circling it. The town obviously took pride in itself, as evidenced by the cheerful flowers and trees that were planted along the streets downtown. She wished there weren't so many vacant storefronts with "For Rent" or "For Sale" signs and empty boxes stacked up inside them that were visible from the road, but that was, unfortunately, becoming a familiar sight.

Still, while the department stores and mom and pop shops of yesterday might be gone, there was still a restaurant on Main recommended by the hotel desk clerk, which she decided to try out for supper. The name, Chester's, didn't make her feel confident in its gourmet selections, but the building was a beautiful turn of the century (that would be the last century, not the current one) brick with original masonry work inside.

She wasn't the only one eating supper out that night, and several of the tables were filled with elderly couples and families with small children. The sturdy wooden tables, covered with thick plastic checkered tablecloths, were far enough apart she didn't feel like she was sitting on top of people and she chose a seat by the window. Always prepared to eat alone, she kept a book in her purse for these occasions, as reading was much better than staring into space or, God forbid, making conversation. However, right now she did kind of feel the need for human companionship.

A teenage boy with long hair pulled back in a ponytail and a wide smile took her order, after telling her it was fried catfish night and that the special came with a piece of pie. (Good enough for her!) Once he left, she settled into her thriller and alternated between watching the people pass by outside and catching up with the heroine in her book. The cars out the window were more exciting, to be honest, and she'd read the same passage four times before she realized she wasn't retaining any information.

When her waiter came back with her sweet tea, he hesitantly stood there for a moment longer than he really needed to and then blurted, "Are you the artist painting the old house?"

"Yes I am," she replied, smiling. With his thin frame and long hair and wire-rimmed glasses, he could have been a younger, more awkward version of Matt. She remembered when he looked a lot like that.

"Yeah, I thought so. My sister works over at Mama Joe's, the restaurant? You eat there sometimes and she told me. I hope that's okay," he said in a rush, the tips of his ears a little red.

News traveled fast in small towns.

"You over there at Windwood Farm?" a young woman at the next table asked. She had three children, all under the age of seven, and was doing her best to keep them in their seats with their food on their own plates while she glanced over at Taryn. The woman was alone and Taryn felt bad for her. She looked like she had her hands full, especially since the youngest kept trying to throw mashed potatoes at what was presumably his sister.

"That's me," she answered, painfully aware that everyone in the room had stopped talking and was watching her. "Hello," she gave the room a general wave.

"You wouldn't catch me going out there by myself, that's for sure," the woman snorted. But she did it with a smile and not in a condescending way, so Taryn smiled back.

"Well, it's really pretty out there," she said diplomatically. "Very peaceful."

"Sure, if you don't count the ghosts," the woman laughed and Taryn was only moderately surprised to see several people in the room nod their heads in agreement.

"So does everyone think it's haunted then?" she asked, figuring that she might as well use the situation to her advantage.

"Anyone who has any sense at all," an elderly gentleman called from the other side of the restaurant. "You don't want to be messing with what goes on in that place, I tell you that. There's some real action out there. I'm seventy-five years old and I seen something there once that I'll never share with nobody."

Taryn was disappointed that he wasn't willing to spill the beans, but the look on everyone's face revealed that they might have had similar stories. "It's an interesting place for sure."

"It's the girl's bedroom that's the worst," the woman confided once everyone went back to their meals and the conversation picked up. "I been up in there, just once, when I was a teenager. I even thought about taking something from there, you know, like a souvenir? I know that's awful, but I was young. There were some keys on the dresser, though, and they were real old. I thought, why not? Nobody needs them now. Minute I touched them, all hell broke loose. I heard a crying and a buzzing and I don't know what all else. I took off out of there like a bat out of hell. Never went ghost hunting again. I don't care what them shows tell you on TV. It's nothing to mess around with."

Taryn shivered, imagining the room the way it looked now, untouched. No wonder nobody had done anything to it. "I heard something similar. What do you think is going on there?" She didn't want to tell her about the pictures, no matter how much she wanted to share it with someone else.

"I think it might be the girl who died in the house. Maybe her spirit is just hanging on and she don't want nobody touching her stuff," the woman laughed. "I don't blame her, I guess. I'm kind of particular about my own. But the whole place just feels sad, you know? Like you want to cry right along with it."

Taryn nodded. "Yes, I know. I talked to someone else about it, too."

"Shame, though," she said as she turned back to her meal. "It's a real pretty place. Could be fixed up. You know, if someone could really live there. The 'Devil's house.' That's what we always called it. Cause only the Devil hisself could stand to live in it."

It wasn't just that the people of Vidalia thought there were ghosts in the house—they all seemed to accept the fact and be okay with it. That was kind of unusual within itself. It was the fact that although almost everyone she'd met so far (okay, all three of them) had some kind of experience with the house, there was a kind of respect for its energy in that they all appeared to be in agreement to the extent that now people simply stayed away.

"The people who lived in the house, they died eighty years ago," she'd pointed out to the mother the night before.

The woman had looked at her like she had two heads. "Oh, that doesn't matter," she said in response. "You grow up hearing about the stories and about the people who lived in a place, they might as well have died yesterday. Don't matter that nobody alive right now never met them. The past ain't really that long ago. It's still alive."

Taryn thought there might be a study somewhere in this idea and if she had more time, she might try to write a grant proposal and find the funds to do it herself. The house and its history was a part of Vidalia and its former residents were as known and talked about now as they probably were eighty years ago. History really did live on, no matter what happened in the meantime.

The "Devil's house." She wondered what the Stokes County Historical Society thought about that. She still resisted the idea of it being evil but it was probably safe to say that most of the people who knew about the house were probably in favor of its reputation. She wondered how they'd feel about Reagan demolishing it. Would they be glad it was gone? Sad they were losing a local landmark? People could be funny about these things. Unlike most local haunted houses, though, Windwood Farm was respected, almost revered for its haunting. That alone set it apart.

When Taryn pulled up into the driveway this time, she didn't get out and walk to the house and go inside. She didn't unload her paints and set up outside in the yard. Instead, she stood in the driveway for a few moments and studied the land. Many of these older families were buried in family plots nearby rather than in local cemeteries. It was possible this family was as well. Scanning the property, she looked for a rise that might indicate a small graveyard and it wasn't long before she saw something that stood out.

Behind the barn, which had seen better days for sure but still stood somewhat regally with its dilapidated roof and with only one door off its hinges, was a knoll with what could be a rusty cow gate peeking through the tall grass. She lamented over the fact she'd worn her sandals and not her boots today, it had stopped raining after all and the ground was dry, but on her way she stopped and picked up a long stick just in case she encountered anything that slithered and hissed. Spiders and ghosts, she had decided she could handle. Snakes? Not so much.

The gravel road that led up to the knoll was well-maintained, probably thanks to Reagan's efforts at developments. The gravel was white and fresh and it was easy to walk on. White powder drifted up and landed on her soft leather sandals with each step she took, coating them with a fine layer. Her legs had already taken on a fine tan that summer and her shoulders felt good in the morning sun. It actually felt nice to be out for a walk and she enjoyed the exercise, despite the fact that the rise was turning out to be more uphill than it had looked from the car. She decided then and there that she needed to get out more and devote more time to physical activity. "Damn, I'm more out of shape than I thought I was," she muttered to herself. "Gotta tone up or something."

It took about ten minutes to reach the knoll and with a few pokes of the stick, she discovered that she was right, it was indeed a gate. It was also padlocked, she saw in disgust. Unfortunately, it wasn't just covered with grass and weeds, it was also covered with brambles and that presented a different problem: bees and thorns. Trying to protect herself from both getting scratched and stung, Taryn ducked and cursed until she had cleared off enough to successfully climb over it and hop to the other side.

Barbed wire enclosed a small yard of what was probably only about eighty square yards, by her estimation. At first, the tall grass and shrubs made it difficult to make anything out and she was afraid she might have been wrong. A few rustles caused her to jump back a few feet, sure that snakes were coming to get her, but it turned out to be a rabbit.

She had freaked herself out long enough and was about to turn around and climb back over the gate when she noticed a glimmer of white reflecting from the sun. It was a small headstone, no more than a foot tall, and mostly covered in black algae from years of neglect and morning glory, but the small patch of white marble that was still visible gave it away. Pulling off a patch of morning glory, the bright blur of flowers blinking merrily at her (how could such pretty little blooms really be considered a weed?) she squatted down at the tiny grave and tried to make out the shallow indentions. There were only three lines of inscriptions:

Clara Joyce Bowen

1903- 1921

Daughter

Well, she figured, that about summed it up. This was the daughter and she was eighteen years old when she died. How much more information did you need? Other than how she died, of course. Taryn felt a little melancholy at her sad little grave. The small headstone, tilted at a weird angle, covered in black gunk, strangled in weeds (albeit pretty ones, but still). Nobody cared. She felt the pangs of a panic attack forming deep inside her, the cold claws starting to scratch at her stomach and rise up into her throat. It wasn't *his* headstone or *his* grave, or *his* cemetery. He didn't have a place. His ashes were scattered over a hillside in eastern Tennessee years ago. He was gone, carried off by the wind. It wasn't the same thing, she told herself. This was Clara. She'd been dead a long time. The world was starting to feel too big around her, too wide, too airy. She grasped the headstone and the moss felt slimy under her hand. The coolness brought her back.

For the next half hour, Taryn did her best to clean off the gravesite. She left the morning glories because they were the only thing close to having decorations or flowers on the grave and she straightened the headstone to as close to upright as best she could. The algae would have to stay until she could find something to clean it off with, maybe vinegar? She was always reading about people cleaning everything with vinegar. She'd have to Google that. At any rate, she figured she'd taken her chances there long enough with the snakes and that now she might be pressing her luck and better head back down to the house and start her real work.

With a little bit of regret, she said goodbye to Clara and started back to the gate. She felt the oddest sensation of someone watching her as she climbed over it, but was too scared to turn around and look back. Instead, she simply scrambled over and then hurried back down the road a little bit faster than she had come up it.

On the way back down, it occurred to her that she hadn't seen any other graves in the graveyard. Why? Why hadn't he been buried with his daughter? Why hadn't *she* been buried with her mother? Had she simply overlooked the other graves? In her zest to clean off the grave, had she just not seen the others, or had they all fallen over and crumbled and been overtaken by nature themselves?

Exploring the graveyard was unsettling to her, but not in the way the activity inside the house had been. She hadn't been scared at the headstone, just sad. There wasn't anything evil near the grave, although she'd certainly felt a presence as she was leaving.

While she was painting the last of the steps leading up to the porch, she couldn't help but think about her own death. Who would be around to clean off her grave, other than the person getting paid to do it? Her grandmother had been dead forever. Her parents were gone and it wasn't the sort of thing they would have thought of, except maybe on the major holidays when they were supposed to because of some sort of traditional obligation. She didn't date, and not because of lack of opportunity (although that had been the case recently) but because she just really couldn't trust herself to. The last few times she'd tried relationships, she'd become so obsessed with the dumbass in question that it had been disastrous, so she'd sworn off men altogether until she was able to pull herself together. A trunk full of self-help books were gathering dust.

Matt. Matt would clean off her grave. The thought gave her comfort.

Or maybe she'd just get cremated and ask him to sprinkle her ashes around the ocean. *Nah,* she wrinkled her nose as she dabbed a spot of white on a column. She wasn't big on water. Not on big bodies of water anyway. Swimming pools were okay, but she wasn't that great of a swimmer. Not that she would care when she was dead, but it should be a place she liked. Something symbolic. That's what people did when they were cremated, right? She just thought the ocean because he lived next to it and the location was convenient for him.

The problem was, there wasn't a place that was meaningful for her. Her grandmother's house had sold. Her apartment was...an apartment. Her parent's house had never been a home for her, and at any rate it sold a long time ago. There was no "family estate." She didn't grow up vacationing anywhere. She'd been working since she was eighteen, and although there were lots of places she liked, she never stayed in one place long enough to get attached to it. The hillside in Tennessee wouldn't do. She hadn't been able to go back. It was his, not hers.

Of course, she did like her Aunt Sarah's place up in New Hampshire. She visited there, once, when she was eight. It was on a lake in the middle of the state, near Conway. She remembered the mountains and a big farmhouse. She couldn't remember much about Sarah herself, other than the fact she'd been kind of quiet and a little bit of a recluse. Her mother called her a hippie. They'd stayed a week and Taryn spent the time running around and climbing trees and playing in the attic with a vague feeling of someone watching her. It wasn't a bad feeling; rather, she kind of liked it. She'd always wanted to go back, but they hadn't. Sarah still sent a card every Christmas, but they hadn't kept in touch much, which was a pity since she was the only family Taryn had.

Taryn sighed. Now she felt depressed. Thinking about family always did that to her. She'd also messed up both the porch and the column and had linseed oil dripping up her elbow and down her toes. Awesome.

Giving it up for the day, she packed it all in and considered the work portion of the day a loss, although the fun part of the day had at least given her a grave and that was something, not to mention the pancakes.

Before getting into her car, however, she had a change of heart and turned back to the house again. It was only a little after two o'clock and there was plenty of day left. She hated to give up that early. "I'm going out of my ever-loving mind," she sighed as she walked back up to the house, the oil slipping through her toes and mixing with the gravel dust. "Only a moron would do this again."

There was no reason why she shouldn't try to go back inside the house, other than the fact that something had tried to scare her out of it the last time she ventured in through the doors. On the other hand, there really wasn't a reason why she should go into the house, except for the need to satisfy her curiosity.

"It's just a house," she said to herself as she stood on the front porch and stared at the door. "It can't hurt me. Ghosts can't hurt me. Whatever is in there has never killed anyone, just scared them. I cannot be scared."

With Miss Dixie hanging around her neck, she opened the door and tentatively placed her foot over the threshold. So far, so good. No scary shadows or screaming or anything other than the sound of her own labored breathing.

The pictures had to happen again. That couldn't have just been a fluke, something only meant to occur once. Why would the house let her see what it once was if it didn't want her to use that knowledge in some way? And no matter how many times she looked at the photos, she just couldn't come up with any possible reason as to why the past was being revealed to her, other than the fact that the house wanted her to know something important.

"I'm listening, I'm here, and my battery is fully charged," she tried to say cheerfully. "So maybe I don't believe in ghosts-*ghosts*, but I believe something is here. Now will you let me see it?"

The house remained quiet, but the stillness seemed to move around her, like a ripple through a wave. The strong scent of decay that accosted her on the first day filled the room and she coughed, trying to force it out of her mouth. It was making her stomach a little queasy.

She wasn't going to go upstairs today—that was just too much—but in the meantime, she'd try to experiment with the downstairs area. Walking steadily through the rooms, she snapped pictures of the crown molding, the mantle, the windows...details she could explain later in case Reagan or someone else showed up and wondered why she kept going inside.

Each time she took a picture, she quickly looked at the LCD screen and was each time disappointed by the fact the display was normal. Nothing was happening.

Feeling like a total failure, she started toward the front door again, but stopped short of putting her hand on the knob. Turning back around and facing the center of the room, she tried to look past the bare floors and plain walls with their peeling paper and imagine the house as it had once been. It might not have been a happy place, but someone tried to make it homey and clean. She imagined an end table, a lamp, a settee, and pictures on the wall. She imagined a fire blazing in the fireplace, its golden tips reflecting light against the walls. She thought about the curtains that hung from the window and the floor rugs that had probably been beaten out on the porch. While she visualized the room in the same way she had imagined every other old place she'd explored in the past, she raised her camera to her face and snapped a picture. Then another.

Still feeling a little defeated, she finally opened the door and went back out into the sunlight. But this time, when she looked at her screen, she was vindicated. In the center of one of the images was an oak coffee table, doilies littering its top and what looked like a family Bible in the center. It was the only thing in the room, but it was a start.

# Chapter 6

"Damn, if you don't mind me saying so, that is one fine painting!" Reagan let out a slow whistle and stood back, his hands on his stomach. Taryn felt her cheeks redden in spite of herself.

"Well, I'm not finished, but thanks."

He was dressed in khaki shorts, a spool shirt, and golf shoes but he still looked every inch a politician. She'd heard rumors that he was going to run for county commissioner. She'd pegged him a politician the minute he'd introduced himself. She wouldn't hold that against him, though, because she couldn't help but like him.

Today he'd brought his wife, a pert slim blonde with a wispy figure and beauty shop hair. She'd pumped her hand with her cold manicured fingers and then gone off toward the shed where she'd said something about gardening tools. Her little summer dress flounced. Taryn had known girls like her in high school; girls that always had perfect hair and perfect skin and always looked in style. Personally, she hadn't been one of those. Her hair had either been frizzy or oily, and at some point, she'd had some kind of weird cowlick that nobody'd been able to explain, not to mention the embarrassing slight overbite that had never gone away and the braces they hadn't been able to afford. She thought of the story Reagan told her about his wife coming here and trying to clean the place up by herself and couldn't imagine it at all.

"So when do you think you'll be finished?" he asked casually, leaning up against his Silverado. It sparkled in the sunlight, virtually dripping water. She could tell it had just been washed. *They must be on their way somewhere,* she thought. Stopping here to what—check on her? Under the guise to pick something up?

"In about a week," she answered only half-truthfully. "But don't worry. My cost is for the painting. I don't work on an hourly basis. I'll be out of your hair in no time."

"Oh, hell," he laughed. "I'm not worried about it. You're doing a great job. The women down there at the Society and the mayor and everyone's going to love it. Take your time. We're not going to get to this for at least another two months. I got held back on another project anyway. You're fine."

Biting her lip, Taryn looked off in the direction of where his wife disappeared and debated on asking him what she really wanted to know. Then, biting the bullet, let it out. "I need to ask you something..."

"Sure, go ahead."

"How much do you really know about this place? I mean, about its history."

"Not a whole lot, I'm afraid. What do you need to know?"

There wasn't anything scary standing here in the cool of the afternoon talking to this perfectly normal-looking man with his perfectly normal society wife getting her gardening tools from the shed and now she felt foolish, but she had to know and this might be her only chance. "I know that it has a reputation for being haunted. What do you know about that? And about the man who lived here? What happened here, Reagan? Do you know anything? Because I've heard things and felt things. And I know it's not in my head. And you said yourself that your wife heard something and felt it."

Looking toward the shed himself, he took a step closer and leaned his head in to her, whispering. "Look, you're not going crazy. And the fact is, I don't know what happened here. Like I told you, the man, Robert was his name, he died in '33. Heart attack or something. He's buried up in the public cemetery. Big old grave. You can't miss it. First big headstone on the right when you first go in. He made sure of that. Folks say that only four people went to the funeral though, that's how much people liked him. You see how big this house is, or was? He died completely in debt. Owed so much money that he died with nothing. Only way he could afford that headstone was because he'd already paid for it. Paid for it when his wife died. Only thing he was able to pay for was keeping this house in his name. Everyone else he owed money to."

"Why was his daughter buried in the backyard? Why wasn't she buried next to them?" Taryn found that she was whispering too, suddenly aware that the breeze died down as if the house, too, might be listening.

"I heard that he didn't give a rat's ass about his daughter. Maybe he lost interest when his wife died. Some men are like that. Me? My daughters are the world to me. My life. But some men, especially back then, who knows. Maybe he wanted sons. Maybe his heart turned black or some shit like that when he lost his wife."

Seeing the look on her face, Reagan frowned. "Oh, hell, what do I know? Maybe not. Maybe he wanted his daughter buried close to him while he was alive?"

The last part was a nice thought, but Taryn didn't think so and it was obvious Reagan really didn't, either.

"And the ghosts?"

"I think it's him," Reagan confided. "I've never seen him myself, but it feels like a man. I heard a scream once. It was primal. Shook me to my soul, it did. It was at night. I come up here to get my tools and I was in one of those upstairs bedrooms. There was a set of keys. I didn't remember seeing them before. I picked them up and I heard something I'll never forget. A scream that—"

"Shook you," she finished for him.

Reagan nodded. "You've heard it, too?"

"Yes, but it sounded to me like it was coming from outside."

"To me, too, but then I heard things flying around downstairs. I got out as fast as I could. My wife, she's heard things she won't even talk about. I threw those keys down on the floor and left. When I came back a week later, they were right back on the dresser."

Reagan looked like he might be about to say more but at that instant his wife appeared around the corner of the house, a bucket full of seeds and gardening tools in her arms and a bright sunny smile on her face. The breeze picked back up again and her hair lifted and blew around her face. "You ready?" she sang.

"As I'll ever be," he smiled and gave her a light peck on the cheek.

"You call me if you need anything," he said as he hopped up in the cab of the truck.

With a wave of her brush, Taryn saw both of them off and went back to work.

Taryn tried not to think about what Reagan had told her as she pushed open the door with a shove and tentatively walked to the foot of the staircase. The broken glass still littered the front steps and porch, but the living room was clear of debris and stone cold quiet. There were no signs that anything had happened on her last visit.

"Hello!" she called. "Yea, it's me! I'm back! Any shenanigans you want to try? Because let's just get them out of your system right now if you do! I'm coming up!"

Bracing herself on the staircase, she waited and listened. Nothing. Taking a gentle step with her right foot, she tried going up one. Again, nothing. So far, so good. Halfway up the stairs, she thought she might have heard a squeak down below and thought about turning around and hoofing it back down, but when she didn't hear anything else, she kept going on.

The bedroom looked exactly as it did the first time she'd been in it. She still couldn't get over how pristine and untouched it was compared to the rest of the house. The bed might have lacked a sheet and bedspread, but it still looked as though it was waiting for someone to come lie down at any moment. A music box sat on the dresser, a drawer opened to reveal a necklace with a charm on it—a horse. It looked like something a child might wear. Articles of clothing were folded up in an open trunk in the corner of the room next to a rocking chair. The entire room was oddly devoid of dust, although there was a faint touch of grime, almost mildew, that settled over it like a blanket. She couldn't see it, but felt it, as though something invisible was touching her skin.

Standing in the middle of the room, Taryn made slow circles in place, taking everything in. It didn't look like anything had been moved in years. There were three pairs of leather shoes next to a wardrobe. She wanted to open the wardrobe and peer inside, but was afraid to. Too many horror movies, and too many bad experiences inside the house already...

A set of skeleton keys with two smaller keys on the key ring was on the dresser. *That must have been what the woman at Chester's was talking about,* she thought, and again marveled at the fact that the keys were still there. Taryn walked over to it and felt compelled to pick it up. It was the only thing in the house she had touched so far and the heaviness of the keys felt odd and foreign in her hands. She'd held the keys for more than a couple of seconds when she looked up and caught her reflection in the mirror.

Moisture eroded the mirror's silver backing over the years and the black distorted her image. She watched her face as it wove in and out of the black spots of the faded reflection and then watched in horror as the bed behind her seemed to move, inch by inch, out from the wall.

Dropping the set of keys with a clang on the floor she turned around just in time to hear a loud scream was not her own. In fact, it seemed to come from outside. The bed stopped moving, but as the scream stopped it was replaced by the sounds of the saddest cries she had ever heard.

She'd heard the word "weep" before, but it was an old-fashioned word and not one she was accustomed to using herself. The way this sound rose and fell throughout the hushed house and seemed to echo through the walls and pierce her heart was the only way she would describe it. This soul crushing sound was *weeping* and it seemed to come from everywhere at once. It was all female and she could do nothing but sink to her knees and join along with it until it was over.

It had been a slight stretch of the truth when she told Reagan it would only be a week before she finished but if she kept up with the momentum she'd experienced today she might be finished sooner than she'd thought. There hadn't been any distractions and at the end of the day she stood back and gazed at her canvas with satisfaction. The oil glistened and even her paintbrushes seemed to be sweating in exhaustion. She was tired, wet with sweat, and dirty but she felt good; invigorated. The porch was almost completed. Of course, that was only a small percentage of the house but it was also one of the most difficult parts since a good majority of the porch was no longer standing, thanks to the collapse. She felt *good*.

She felt the vibrations of the car in the driveway before she heard it. It was so rare that a vehicle passed by that the stir of the air currents was enough to shift the atmosphere and change the mood. Shielding her eyes from the glare of the sun, she turned around and looked down the drive. An old model Caddy slowly maneuvered the winding, narrow drive and pulled up behind her. A tall, thin woman with short cropped gray hair in a blue polyester shirt and gray slacks unfolded herself from behind the wheel and made her way to Taryn with the help of a cane. Taryn recognized her as Priscilla as soon as she started speaking. She would know that whiskey/cigarette voice anywhere.

"I'm sorry to interrupt you, dearie, but I just had to come and see how you're doing out here all by yourself. We're all just so excited to have you here!" She said this all in a rush as she engulfed Taryn in a hug, nearly knocking her paints to the ground. She had a good six inches on Taryn's 5'2" frame and she was instantly overcome by the scent of magnolias and Marlboros.

Before Taryn could respond, Priscilla clapped her hands together and gasped. "Why, that is absolutely amazing! Just look at that! Lawd! That looks just like the house itself! They're just going to love it!"

"I'm not finished, of course," Taryn stammered. "There's still a lot of work to do..."

"Oh of course, of course," Priscilla assured her, bringing her fingers close to the painting and then snatching them away in awe. "It almost looks like a photograph! And the light...Are you sure there's not a light bulb behind it?"

Taryn laughed. "I'm sure. I try to capture the light as best I can."

"It's better than I ever dreamed it would be. I think it looks better than the real thing!"

"I was about to stop and have a break," Taryn lied. But she certainly couldn't work now. "Would you like to sit down on the porch and take a rest and have a soda or some lemonade? I have a cooler in my trunk."

"I'll have a Pepsi or something of that nature if you have one," Priscilla smiled. "It's a hot one today."

After she got them settled Taryn resigned herself to the fact that it might take a while before her momentum was back on track again. "I told Reagan it would be about a week before I finished, but it might be longer. Is that okay?"

"Oh," Priscilla waved. "That's no problem. Don't worry about him. He's probably forgotten you're even here. And we certainly don't mind. We're just happy you're doing it! I am thrilled to see this old place coming alive!"

With the words "coming alive" Taryn couldn't help but shudder a little, despite the fact that it was the same phrase she often used to describe her services herself.

"I wanted to ask you something about the family who lived here the longest, the Bowens?"

"Oh, yes, Robert Bowen," Priscilla nodded.

"Where did they come from? Before moving here, I mean."

111

Priscilla closed her eyes before answering. "Let me think...Oh yes. Well, he was from the county north of us. I don't know anything about his people. But his wife, she was from the other side of the river, over in Clark. Same county. About ten miles from here. They lived with her family for the first couple of years and then bought this house and moved here. I reckon to be close to her family. Family was important back in those days, more so than now. Now, everyone's spread from here to yonder. Back then, though, you wanted to stay close, stay in clans. Watch out for each other."

"Why not to be closer to his family? I mean, why not move to his county?"

"Oh, well, I believe her family was the one with the money. And it was more than likely that it was her daddy that bought them this house and farm. Robert died deeply in debt; that is widely known. He farmed this land, but he wasn't highly successful at it. Her daddy died not long after they bought this farm and it is my understanding that whatever money he left her Robert probably squandered quickly."

Taryn nodded her head. "So they lived here in a nice house, and had a lot of land, but they weren't wealthy."

"Not by any means," Priscilla agreed. "Now, the family on the other side of them, *that* was another story. They were the richest family in town. I'm sure that rubbed Robert the wrong way. Robert died a poor man, though. And his poor wife and daughter both died young. Just tragic, really. And now this poor house is going to be torn down. Just tragic all the way around."

With care, Taryn wrapped her brushes up and cautiously slipped her canvas into the back of the car, careful not to let it touch anything. The last thing she needed was to get paint all over the seats. The waxed paper and old sheets protected most of the upholstery, but she'd had accidents before, as the splatters attested. She considered them character, but tried not to let it become a habit.

Taryn was surprised to discover it was almost six o'clock by the time she collapsed her easel and loaded it into the trunk. She had lost complete track of time. She packed everything up quickly, though, and was about to open her car door and slip inside when the air around her rapidly changed. Where it had been mild and even a little cool before, it became hot and stifling in a matter of seconds. Still. She found herself gasping for breath as the heat settled in around her, climbing down her throat and filling her nostrils. Like she did on the staircase a week earlier, she gasped for breath and fell back against the car, sliding down to the ground. Fumbling for her keys, with one hand she clutched at her throat and with the other and tried in vain to find the key that would start her engine, but her fingers wouldn't quite work properly. They seemed to have swollen and wanted to stick together.

Off in the distance, a noise started. It was low at first, a faint thud. It sounded as though something might have fallen. She thought she might have imagined it. The heat was so intense

113

waves of heat shimmered in the air and the house itself appeared to glow. She dropped the keys on the ground and shielded her eyes to peer at the house and get a better look and, as she did, the screams began. There was no mistaking *this* sound. She knew screaming when she heard it. It was loud and strong and most definitely male. And the voice was in trouble.

Getting to her feet, Taryn rain the direction of the house but stopped short when she reached the porch. The sounds weren't coming from the house; the scream was coming from *under* her feet, from under the ruins, in fact. Stopping, she sank to her feet and put her ear to the ground, listening, the horrible heat piercing into her and sweat rolling down her face in streaks and gathering onto her stomach and back. There was nothing. Now the sounds were coming from her left, from her right, like an echo. They were everywhere. As loud as they were, they faded in and out, growing louder and fainter with each shout.

Taryn ran back and forth across the yard, pressing her ear to the ground, but each time she thought she found the source, it moved. "What do you want?" she yelled. "I can't find you! What do you want?"

Finally, in exhaustion, she dropped to the ground and cried. "What do you want," she beat her fists on the ground, sweat pooling around her. Choking and gagging on hot air, dizzy and faint, she sobbed. "What do you want..."

As she cried, the screaming slowly died down as well. The blistering heat was replaced by the cool breeze and it soothed Taryn's skin as it lifted her hair and swept over her, like a balm.

114

She cried and cried, not only out of frustration but for her own perceived lack of sanity and for a whole list of other things as well. She was tired, her head was throbbing, she missed her grandmother, and she didn't know what to do.

Soon, another sound joined her own cries. She became aware of the sobbing from the upstairs window almost immediately and as the weeping emanated through the afternoon breeze the two women cried together, each one in their own time, each one for their own reasons, and neither one able to help the other.

"*Under* the house? Well, that's different," Matt mused.

"Not just under the house," Taryn explained, taking a bite of her McChicken, much to Matt's disgust (he really did need to go up there and make her some decent food). "More like under the *ground*. At least I think it was. It kept moving. And damn, it was fucking hot."

Matt cringed. He wasn't big on her language, either. But he'd learned to live with it. "The obvious answer is that someone is buried either under the ground or under the house, right?"

"Of course," Taryn shrugged. "I guess they'll figure that out when they tear up the house. If there's a mystery, Shaggy, then it will be solved."

Matt slouched on his futon in his shorts and T-shirt with his skinny white legs glowing in the pale lamp light, ate his gumbo out of a Pottery Barn bowl, and tried not to imagine what Taryn looked like in her nightgown. It was difficult. The first thing she'd said when she'd answered the phone was, "I just put on my nightgown," and the rest of the conversation was just too hard to focus on.

"So the daughter died of tuberculosis—" Matt began.

"So Reagan told me when I first met him," Taryn interrupted him, "but Tammy-the-waitress said her granny thought that was suspicious. Apparently people in town weren't really sure that's what happened. It checked out with the coroner, I guess, but other people thought something else might have happened."

"Okay, so Clara-the-daughter may or may not have died of TB, but she apparently died of something that looked natural. And someone, we're guessing a man, is buried under the ground. Or at least died under the ground. And we don't think it's Robert-the-bad-dude since he's buried in the local cemetery. Wait, are we SURE it isn't Robert-the-bad-dude?"

"What do you mean?" Taryn asked, popping a fry into her mouth. Matt would be mortified if he knew she was also drinking a large mocha. He just did not understand the beauty of McDonalds at midnight.

"Okay, if people really didn't like him and hardly anyone showed up at his funeral, what if some folks came out to his house, killed him, or didn't kill him, and buried him under his house. What if his casket is empty? What if they buried him alive? What if he murdered his daughter and years later someone found out about it and they sent a lynch mob out there to get him and his whole funeral was just a farce?"

Chills ran up and down Taryn's arms. "Oh my God, Matt. That's it! That's *perfect*. That's got to be it. That's why there's so much anger in the house. And they said he died in debt. He owed money to everyone in the county, he killed his daughter, and eventually someone was bound to find out. Someone, or a bunch of people, came out and killed him. They buried him in the front yard, part of the house eventually collapsed on that part of the yard, and now his ghost haunts the house and is trapped in it. And his daughter's ghost haunts the house because she was also murdered there. You got it!"

"Well," Matt grinned, "I do read a lot."

Taryn wasn't sure why she didn't feel better.


Long after she'd hung up the phone and settled down into her red flannel nightgown, picked up at some secondhand store along the way because she always shopped cheap and always froze to death no matter where she stayed, she let her mind drift back to the first time she really knew something wasn't right.

Obviously, the pictures of Windwood Farm startled her. Who wouldn't be taken aback by them? She wasn't crazy. She'd about had a heart attack when she'd seen them pop up on her computer screen and she'd looked at them a hundred times since then, going over their details. And she'd taken even more since the first day, although her images since then had all been normal.

But Matt knew her truth, her real truth.

This wasn't the first time something had happened.

When Taryn was six and still living in Nashville, she'd lived in a perfectly normal subdivision on the west side of town. New houses were being built and the kids in her neighborhood liked to play in them, despite the fact their parents told them to stay out of them. Back in those days, it was perfectly safe to ride your bikes after dark, even in her neighborhood in Nashville. It felt more like a small town back then and everyone watched out for each other and she played with a group of kids that felt like a posse. They stayed out together until suppertime until someone stepped out on their front porch and cried for a kid to come in to eat and they all scattered. It was never one of her parents, but she'd always scatter with the rest of them, never wanting to stay out by herself.

One evening, a new kid joined the posse. He was skinny with dark hair and dark eyes and glasses. A head taller than the rest of them, the others made fun of him because he instantly started talking about the solar system and bugs. He introduced himself as Matt. She liked him immediately and felt a kinship with him but wasn't sure why. When the others wanted to pick on him, she threatened to beat them up, even though she was nearly a foot shorter and a grade below most of them.

A family had just moved out of a house on the street and the front door was standing wide open. It was a big house and this was a change. Normally, they explored houses that were just being built, but this one was different: it was already finished. Why not explore it? Taryn wasn't sure. After all, wasn't that more like breaking into it? It had a roof and everything. Matt felt the same way, but it was his first day in the neighborhood and he wanted to fit in.

Giving in to everyone else, and not wanting to ruin his chances at making new friends, he talked Taryn into going along with the gang. Silently, the ten of them crept into the foyer and sneaked through the rooms. It was a large home, nearly 4,000 square feet. Taryn didn't know the family who lived there before. They'd had two young children but the girls were toddlers, too young to play with her. She'd only seen the wife taking them in and out of the car. Once, she'd waved to Taryn but she'd looked nervous and frazzled. Not approachable. Taryn's dad called her "skittish." She thought the husband always seemed mad. She didn't know what he did for a living, but his voice was always loud and he had a car phone. He was the only person she knew who did. It had only taken them one day to move and they'd hired a moving company to do it.

The house was impeccably clean. There wasn't a single stain on the carpet or walls. Everything smelled like bleach and it stung Taryn's eyes a little bit. She mentioned this to Matt and he went into a long speech about how bleach was often used by cleaning companies to help eliminate odors, especially after a family moved and the carpets needed deodorizing. Taryn was impressed by his knowledge, especially since he was only eight.

Eventually, Taryn and Matt got separated and he ended up going upstairs where there was an actual hot tub in the bedroom. She found a little door that led down to the basement. There, she discovered another small staircase that she thought would take her outside. Instead, it took her to a small room where she found another even smaller door. Curious, she tried to open it. When she did, she was startled to see a little girl lying on the floor. It was one of the little girls who lived there. She was wearing a flowered dress and her hair was covered in red paint. "Are you okay?" she asked. But the little girl's eyes were closed. The room was almost black, except for a faint glow that hovered over the child's face and body. She was motionless.

Taryn suddenly had chills on her arms and legs. Her grandmother would say that a goose walked on her grave. Something wasn't right. Why would the little girl be here when her family had moved? "Do you want me to call someone?"

As she watched in horror, the little girl seemed to actually sink down into the ground until all that was left was the floor. Even the glow disappeared. Tentatively, Taryn reached out and touched the floor and discovered that it was hard, packed dirt that was cool to the touch. With a little shriek, she ran out and up the stairs and flew out of the house.

When she got home, she told first her parents, who didn't believe her, and later her grandmother, who did. They all chalked it up to a combination of food poisoning and bad dreams. Her parents talked to the other parents, however, and that put a stop to the exploring. The other children blackballed her from the neighborhood expeditions and from that day forward, she only played with Matt, which was really just fine and dandy with the two of them. She'd never gotten much out of playing with the rest of the lot, anyway.

Years later, a developer bought most of that subdivision and tore down a great portion of those houses and built condominiums. They were awfully surprised to find the body of a two year old child buried under the house. Taryn, on the other hand, unfortunately, was not surprised. That incident taught her something, however. There were certain things one should just keep to one's self. After that day she rarely shared anything with anyone but Matt. And most things she just preferred thinking were in her head. It was easier that way.

# Chapter 7

The call from the Stokes County Historical Society was not a surprise. Frankly, she'd been expecting something a little sooner. An Edna Washington, with a thin, kind of warbled voice, apologized for her lateness and asked if she could come in this morning. Apparently, the Society only met on Saturdays. Taryn planned on going to Lexington and walking around the big bookstore she'd heard good things about, but resigned herself to spending the afternoon with the ladies of the Society. After all, it was their grant money that was paying her. And if she didn't then, she was just going to have more of them wandering out to the job site, poking their noses into her painting.

She paid special attention to her attire. No short-shorts or wet hair. Makeup. Older women appreciated it when your clothes matched and you didn't show too much skin. She didn't normally dress raunchy, but she always tried not to let her bra straps show or her underwear hang out when she was around them. She really wasn't a jean shorts or sweatshirt kind of gal anyway, but she was likely to throw on whatever was handy and these days she hadn't had the chance to get to the laundromat.

The Stokes County Historical Society was housed in a doublewide trailer at the end of Main Street. Two wheelbarrows on either side of it held violet pansies. Window boxes were full of flowers that Taryn couldn't name, but they were certainly colorful.

She wasn't sure whether she should knock or go on in, but while she was deciding, a thin, reedy gray-headed woman opened the door for her and ushered her inside. An air conditioner was going full blast and she was met with a glaring fluorescent light and a plate full of chocolate chip cookies. "We've got lunch ready for you, too," someone called from behind a partition as she was led to an overstuffed couch.

The room was large with a big conference table and there were about a dozen women, mostly elderly, seated around it like they were the Knights of the Round Table. Each one had a photo album or scrapbook in front of them, studying it with serious expressions on their faces, many taking notes and muttering under their breaths. Some were even speaking into small tape recorders. One lone man was at a computer, staring at a long list of names.

The walls were adorned with posters, photographs, historical maps, and charts. Other than the one partition that separated what she assumed was the kitchen from the rest of the room, the rest of the walls were removed so that the double wide was one big space. Glass display cases filled the area and she could see coins, tools, and other memorabilia from days gone by lining the walls. It was actually pretty interesting and she wouldn't mind looking around, but before she could get up, a plate full of sandwiches, cookies, and something that resembled a casserole was placed in her lap by the same woman who showed her in. "Eat," she demanded. "You need some meat on those bones."

"Okay," she whimpered. After all, she wasn't one to turn down food.

"Girls, Leonard, she's here."

With that, all the women looked up, as if on cue. The man slowly turned away from his computer gazing. The books all snapped shut and the tape recorders were turned off. Taryn closed her mouth around the sandwich and then stopped. Was she expected to give a speech now? She hadn't prepared anything.

A pleasant looking woman with snowy white hair smiled kindly at her. "Priscilla says your painting is beautiful. She's sorry she can't be here today, but she's with Sally at the hospital. We're all taking shifts. She says it's just what we are looking for. We can't wait to see it. We've wanted to know what the rest of that house would look like for years. We saw what you did with the governor's mansion...just breathtaking."

Taryn swallowed. "Thank you," she replied, sincerely.

"I'm Shirley. Are you liking it here in Vidalia?" This came from a heavyset woman in a bright pink polka-dot dress and green sandals who was systematically making her way through a large glass of sweet tea. She vigorously nodded her head as she asked her question, as if she already knew the answer.

"Yes, I am, although I haven't been able to see much of the town. I've been working a lot," Taryn said with regret. "It's very pretty, though."

"What do you think of the house? Aren't the stones beautiful?" The question was from a little woman who really looked to be no more than a child. She was thin and her features small, like a bird. Her face peered over from the top of the table and the horn-rimmed glasses that perched on the edge of her nose made her looked as though she was playing dress up. Taryn couldn't help but smile.

"Well, it's interesting...."

"Ha, she's talking about the ghosts," Shirley snorted.

"Now, Shirley," the bird admonished.

"Don't you 'now Shirley' me," Shirley chastised. "We all know it is."

"Do you really think it is?" Taryn asked with feigned innocence.

"Oh, honey," the ancient gentleman with deep blue veins running through his hands and liver spots on his arms spoke softly to her. "There's no need to be like that with us. We all know it is. We'd be shocked if you hadn't seen or heard something. It's probably that son of a bitch himself doing it. There are so many tragedies in this town, the whole damn place is haunted."

Everyone laughed good-naturedly and for a while the mood was relaxed and the matter was forgotten. Taryn got caught up with stories about Vidalia and the time during the Depression and later during the baby boom. They were also interested in her stories as well and she found herself telling them about places she had painted in the past. There were rarely audiences as captivated as those who belonged to a historical society and with these folks she felt amongst kindred spirits. After all, they shared a love of old homes and buildings and didn't want to see anything torn down any more than she did. She might not have enjoyed genealogy like they did, she wasn't even sure who her great grandparents were (to this group's horror) but they could all agree that there ought to be an organization like PETA for the ethical treatment of old homes and structures.

She wanted to ask them Matt's theory about Robert being murdered but it just never felt appropriate to bring it up. Perhaps if she could get one of them on their own, but in front of the whole group...

She was talking to Shirley and in the middle of eating her fourth cucumber sandwich when she heard someone mumble, "And, of course, let's not forget about what happened to little Donald Adkins..."

"Wait, what happened to Donald? Who's Donald?" Taryn interrupted. She realized she let herself daydream and was lost in thought. She'd eaten far too much and enjoyed herself a lot more than she'd thought she would. The room really was full of a cast of characters and she'd been craving human companionship more than she'd realized.

"Donald," the older gentlemen whose name was Leonard continued. "Was a young fellow who lived not too far from Windwood Farm. The next farm over, actually. He disappeared in, oh, I think about 1921, I'd say. Just a few years before I was born. I was born in 1939. My pappy remembered it and used to tell me about it. Was a big story back then, of course, because people didn't just up and disappear a lot. Went out to tend to the horses and never come home. There were some drifters around and some folks say they got 'im and kilt 'im. I don't know about that but they never found his body. Never knew what happened to 'im. 'Course, he could've runned off. His folks never thought so, though. He was a good boy, bound for college in a year and that was a big deal back then. They grieved themselves to death, first his mama and then his daddy, just a year apart."

"Oh," Taryn said. "That's really sad. Was that at the same time Clara from Windwood Farm died, too?"

"Yes it is," Shirley agreed. "Same year. A sad year for young folks. Tuberculosis got many young folks, and old folks, that year as well. Lots of deaths. Then the stock market crashed a few years later and that took care of a lot of folks around here, too. That was the start of the decline of Vidalia, though, the early 1920s."

Seeing a window of opportunity, Taryn pounced. "Do you really believe that TB is what killed Clara?"

A penetrable silence filled the room and it wasn't hard to notice that several of the older folks visibly squirmed. "Well, of course, it was the official cause of death," someone volunteered.

"And it was what her mother died of," someone else answered. "And I know that for a fact. My own grandmother saw to her care and saw her waste away. No doubt about that. You know, that was before the antibiotics was around. Not a lot of treatment for TB. There were them sanatoriums, but the treatments usually weren't much but sunshine and fresh air."

"Took out a lung when they could," Shirley offered.

"True," Leonard agreed. "But Mrs. Bowen, she stayed right here. Didn't leave home. Some folks didn't. It was risky and, of course, nobody wanted to go near 'em for fear of getting it themselves but a lot of 'em wanted to stay home if they could."

"Why wouldn't she and Clara have gone away?" Taryn asked.

"No money," Shirley answered. "Or else nobody knew they were sick. Sometimes it came up on them so fast they were nearly dead before anybody knew they had it. That happened sometimes. Not often, but tuberculosis sometimes acted like other things. Folks get scared, hide it, pretend like nothing was wrong. Be faint and weak and sick until they couldn't hide it any longer and then there wasn't nothing to do but die."

They all sat in silence, each one of them lost in their thoughts. Taryn wasn't so sure she didn't blame them. She'd heard about some of the sanatoriums, especially the big one in Louisville, and how nice they actually were. But nothing beat being at home. She liked to think that if it was her time to go she could have the choice and control about where it would be.

Still, that particular part of the conversation seemed to be over. When she saw she wasn't going to get any more than that, she pressed a different angle. "Well, what about Robert? Is it possible maybe he didn't die of a heart attack? That maybe it was something else?"

"Like what, dear?" Shirley asked gently.

Now it was Taryn's time to squirm. "Like murder, maybe?"

Everyone laughed. "Ha ha, everyone's thought that!" Leonard guffawed. "You think someone didn't want to kill him? They was all standing in line! He owed money to everyone! Even the coroner! But no, dear, it was a heart attack, plain and simple.

Even took a picture of the dead body. We've got it somewhere here if you'd like to see it. They did that back then you know..."

Taryn felt her heart sink.

"Why did they..."

The woman whom she had come to think of as the "bird woman" smiled at her. "It's just a common thing to take pictures at funerals around here. And, with so many enemies, some people just wanted proof that he was really dead and not trying to get out of paying his debts. I know, honey, it might sound morbid, but he wasn't, let's say, the most popular gentleman in the county. We didn't bring you in here to paint his house because we were fans of him, just a fan of the architecture."

She replayed the conversation from the group at the Stokes County Historical Society over and over in her head and something about it just wasn't sitting right for her. As nice as it would have been (okay, as gruesome as it would have been), Robert really was dead and in the grave in the Vidalia public cemetery. She had seen the picture taken at his public service. He'd been a portly, sallow fellow in death. But he'd definitely been dead as a doornail. Whatever that meant. He wasn't buried beneath the house, either the standing part or the crumbled part. Someone still may have murdered the old dude, but he was where he should be. That didn't mean he wasn't haunting the house, of course, but it did mean their first theory could fly out the window.

129

Now there was something else bothering her, though. There wasn't any evidence that pointed to the fact that Donald Adkins' disappearance had anything to do with what had gone on at Windwood Farm. In fact, there wasn't really anything to prove that anything other than simple tragedy had happened at Windwood Farm at all. All of the deaths checked out. Clara and her mother almost certainly died of TB. Robert died of a heart attack or something natural and was buried where he was supposed to be. She and Matt had been wrong.

But she still had a feeling. Taryn trusted her gut more often than she trusted logic.

There was no reason to think Donald's disappearance had anything to do with Windwood Farm. Nobody at the Historical Society could give her an exact date for his disappearance, only that was "sometime late in the fall" but they pointed her to the newspaper office. The Stokes County Daily had once been the Stokes County Herald and issues back then were sent out once a week instead of every day. Shirley assured her, though, that they should have the 1920s editions on microfiche. She, herself, had perused the old issues when doing her genealogy.

Taryn decided to start there.

She hated giving up such a beautiful morning when she should be out at the house, painting, but she knew if she didn't get this out of her system, it would nag at her. Since leaving the meeting, she'd barely been able to think about anything else, but that was almost a welcomed relief. In fact, she'd actually experienced a good night's sleep the night before. Most nights, she needed the help of at least one Tylenol PM, especially since she'd developed a nagging headache a few months back and it only seemed to be worsening in this heat, but last night she'd drifted off like a baby and hadn't had a single bad dream. Matt sent her a text message and reminded her that a special was coming on about the Titanic, something she would usually make sure not to miss, but she'd slept right through it.

Before starting out that morning, she made herself a jug of sweet tea and filled it full of ice using the machine in the hallway. She narrowly missed being accosted by the businessman she'd met in the pool the week before (what was *he* still doing there?) but she slipped out through the side door before he could catch up with her. She still wasn't up for having lunch or dinner with anyone yet and he'd looked at her expectantly.

The clerk at the front desk of the newspaper office was expecting her, thanks to a phone call from Shirley, and immediately greeted Taryn warmly and offered her something to drink. Taryn was anxious to get started, though, and with her tea in hand she told the friendly clerk that she was ready for action.

The newspaper office was in a large, squat building downtown that had once been somewhat of a grand hotel. As the clerk led her back through the offices to the archives room Taryn still saw remnants of the once glorious past in the marble flooring, detailed cornices, and original woodwork. The printing room was formerly a ballroom of sorts, the clerk told her, and featured live music and dancing most Saturday nights during the summer. But that was many, many years ago, before the Depression. Now, it

131

was dusty and the floors were streaked with ink and there was a slight musty smell to the air. It wasn't entirely unpleasant, but the preservationist in her mourned for the building it must have once been.

Taryn asked for the issues from August until December of 1921. "Sometime in the late fall" could mean anywhere from the middle of summer to Christmas. Luckily, since the paper had only been put out once a week back then, she wouldn't have too many issues to sort through. She just hoped that Donald's disappearance was considered big news for the time so that she wouldn't have to go searching through all of the pages.

Once she was set up and got started, drifting back through Vidalia in 1921 actually proved to be fun, despite the fact that she had zero ties to the town or to the people. In particular, she loved the advertisements, and the stories which were all a little bucolic and sentimental by today's standards. Very little national news was reported, but livestock reports and town gossip took center stage. She could have easily gotten lost in the history of the time period, just by reading through the local stories. What the reporters considered to be important and newsworthy said as much about the culture of the town as it did about the time period. For instance, even though there was a brutal murder in the next county over in late August, it barely got four sentences at the bottom of the second page of that edition. The cover story, however, was all about the county fair and which winners would be moving on to the state levels. Considerable pride was evident and shone through in the writing of the article, especially in regards to the livestock.

She could have spent a lot longer reading through each and every edition but she had to remind herself why she was really there. With time short on her hands, she did her best to read quickly and move on when she didn't find what she was looking for.

There were quite a few stories about the Fitzgeralds, both Jonathan and his sister Lucy showed up more than once for their social status and volunteer efforts, but it wasn't until the middle of November that she finally found what she was looking for. The article was on the front page, though it wasn't the feature story, and the headline claimed "Local boy missing."

## Local Boy Missing

*Donald Adkins, of Sally Ann Farm, was reported missing last week by his father, George. Donald was last seen feeding the cattle at 6:00 pm on November 17th. When he didn't return, a search commenced, but Donald was unable to be located. If anyone has any information on his whereabouts, please contact the police.*

His story didn't appear again until December 21st of that year. This time it was the feature and the headline read: "Arrest Made in Disappearance."

## Arrest Made in Disappearance

*An arrest has been made in the disappearance of local resident, Donald Adkins. Stewart Evans, of Columbus, Ohio, was arrested near Fitz on Saturday morning. Stewart, who has been living on and off in Stokes County for the past six months, was taken in for public intoxication. Once contained, he admitted to not having a permanent home and claimed he had been staying in "abandoned houses and railroad cars." When questioned about the disappearance of Donald, he at first denied any wrongdoing but later said he "might have seen him." Evidence suggests that Evans might have had a hand in the young man's departure.*

Stewart Evans, drifter that he was, never got to stand trial for the disappearance of Donald, however, because a week later it was reported that he passed away in a jail cell in Vidalia from an apparent heart attack, most likely brought on by drinking (according to popular opinion).

Taryn was excited, and a little disappointed by the news. Of course, it was highly possible that this fellow from out of town had something to do with Donald's disappearance. It was also highly probable that blaming the vanishing on a drunk that nobody knew was the easy route to take. So the stories really left her with more questions than answers. "Donald, Donald, Donald," she murmured, "What happened to you?" The thing was, nobody was really even sure he was dead. The poor vagrant was arrested on suspicion of a crime that might not have even taken place to begin with.

There wasn't any news of Clara's death, however. A glance at the time told her that the office would close in less than ten minutes so she wrapped everything up and gathered her belongings. At the front desk, she stopped and talked to the clerk, a young woman who was busy reading a paperback romance.

"Thanks for letting me look," she said.

The woman put down her book and smiled. "Did you find what you were looking for?"

"Sort of, but I was wondering if there was a way to look up obituaries. If that was something that I could do quickly," she added. "I've got the name and year, I just need the date."

"We have access to the office of Vital Statistics," the girl answered. "Shouldn't take more than a second."

She got up and walked over to a row of computers against the wall. "What's the name?"

"Clara Bowen, death year 1921."

With a flurry of fingers, the girl typed it into the computer and then waited. "I'm here for my internship. This actually helps me. It's always quiet on Saturdays and looking this up is just one more thing I can report having done."

"Glad to help," Taryn laughed. "I might have more later. If I do more digging."

"Oh, here it is. Clara Bowen." The girl leaned down and looked into the screen. "Says here she died on November 20, 1921."

With a heavy heart, Taryn traveled down the two lane road, past Windwood Farm, past the oak and maple trees that led to Sally Anne Farm, home of the late Donald Adkins. Now, more than ever, Taryn suspected there was a mystery on hand. Why she was the one who felt like she should solve it, she wasn't sure.

Donald might be the key.

"Are you sure you're up for something like this?" Matt asked her the night before. He'd been tentative in his question, gentle. He knew not to push at her too hard, but he was worried about her.

Taryn sat on her bed, the slippery generic hotel blanket under her. She stared at her painting—it needed more work. She just couldn't concentrate on it. The last time she'd been sidetracked was almost six years ago. The accident had happened then. Andrew and his car. For four years they'd been a team, the architect and the artist, traveling together and bringing the past alive to their clients. Ever since that job in Mississippi with the plantation home, when he'd heard the music inside the mansion, she'd known there was something about him that was special. Historical architecture had been his calling. She had been his passion. The damn Camaro had been his vice. Now she worked alone.

"I'm fine, Matt," she assured him. "This is important to me. I don't know why it's happening, but it's important. You know, for the first time in a long time, I actually feel like I'm a part of the thing that I'm bringing alive for everyone else. I'm involved in it."

"That's a little of what I'm afraid of," he said worriedly.

"But I feel okay," she said truthfully. "I feel like I'm getting somewhere. Donald, Clara—these people are starting to feel real to me now. And not just in my imagination. I'm actually starting to see them and feel them. I think I'm supposed to do this and put this together. Maybe that's why I was supposed to take this house, to figure this out." She wasn't sure that she was explaining it well, but *she* knew what she meant. Sort of.

"Yeah, well, if you ever start feeling like you've bit off more than you can chew, then let me know. I know people."

The Sally Anne Farm was more than two hundred years old, making it slightly older than Windwood. The house was a simple log cabin at one point, but was now a sprawling Victorian structure that had been added onto over the years with gables and more modern features that made it look like something out of the Addams family. It wasn't to her taste, although it had a Gothic feel that made it look a little scary. She appreciated the southern horror vibe that was fitting to the mood she felt.

The gate was open and bits of grass were poking up through the gravel in the long driveway. It hadn't been repaved in what looked like years so her car leapt along, giving her jolts as she made her way toward the house, her ponytail bouncing up and down. The folks at the Stokes Historical Society told her the descendants of the original family lived in it, but didn't have any money to speak of, that was lost years ago. The current couple worked as school teachers. It was after five o'clock now and a Saturday anyway. Someone was bound to be home.

One of those wooden swing set monstrosities with a seesaw and garish yellow slide was in the backyard and clashed with the architectural "style" of the house. A green John Deere motorized child's car was upturned on its side beside it. A sandbox was collecting water by the front porch. A cat was currently using it as a litter box. She parked her car next to a gray minivan with a rusted tail pipe and first rang the doorbell and then knocked on the door, just in case. Seconds later, a small dog began barking, followed by the shrieks of a toddler and the cries of a young boy. She was met by a frazzled-looking young woman sporting short cropped auburn hair and holding a crying baby.

"I'm sorry," Taryn apologized, feeling stupid for not calling or something first. The young women looked wild eyed and panicked rather than scared and Taryn wondered if she should offer to take the baby or the dog. "I just came to ask you some questions about the house and your family, or your husband's family..." She could barely hear herself talk over the dog and baby.

"You'll want me then..." she screamed over the noise, almost in relief. "JIMMY!"

Within moments, a young man in cutoff jeans came to the door—shoeless—and conferred with the woman. He smiled at Taryn, then took the baby and gently pushed the dog away from the door. The woman eased herself away and gingerly stepped out onto the porch.

"I am so sorry," Taryn said again. "I'm trying to get some information about this house and the people who used to live here. I'm doing some work on Windwood Farm and just talked to the Historical Society...Hi, I'm Taryn."

"Melissa," the young woman said warmly. She was about twenty-eight, Taryn would guess, and average height and build. She wore a pair of navy blue shorts and her short hair swung around her face in a sleek rain. Her gray T-shirt had a dark stain down the front, but her toenails were painted pink inside her sandals and her lipstick matched. She carried a bright, sunny smile and big blue eyes and Taryn instantly liked her. "Actually, I'm just excited to get out of the house. Want to sit down on the swing? And don't worry about not calling. I've lost my charger anyway. And a few minutes of peace and quiet? This is like a vacation to me!"

It was nice sitting on the front porch swing with a view of the valley around them and Taryn felt a gentle rapport with the stranger. Bees buzzed around them and she could almost forget why she had come out there in the first place.

Melissa kicked off the swing and started a rhythm as she began talking. "My great, great, great grandfather built this place so it's been in my family a long time. Of course, back then it was just a one room cabin. It was almost five hundred acres, too. Now we just have a little over one hundred acres. We like it, though. Hard to keep up, of course. And it's a big house. Sally Anne was his wife," she said conversationally.

139

"It's beautiful out there," Taryn said sincerely. It didn't have any of the oppression that Windwood Farm suffered from. The woods didn't look as menacing and dark on this side, even though they were obviously the same ones that backed up to Windwood. The barns out in the distance were well maintained and their red paint shone in the afternoon sun. A couple of horses grazed peacefully in the fields.

"Our sons love to ride, even though the oldest is only seven. I grew up here. Wouldn't live anywhere else. I suspect you want to know about my great Uncle Donald, though. That's probably why the women down there sent you here. That's what most folks want to know about," Melissa smiled.

"Yes, I'm sorry."

Melissa shrugged. "It's funny, isn't it? I mean, it was such a long time ago, but when it comes to tragedy and family, it might as well have happened yesterday. I mean, I didn't know him and you didn't know him, but here we are, talking about it like it's all recent events and relevant to today." Melissa smiled because it was all true.

Taryn smiled as well. "That's true about the past I guess. It's never too far away. You just can't really escape it. It's one of the reasons I think I was called to painting it. Sometimes I feel more connected to the past than I do to the present. I'm a painter, by the way, an artist. I paint the past."

"I know who you are," Melissa said. "I Googled you when I heard you was coming in. You do nice work. And I think it's great, what you're doing over there. That old place is kind of creepy, but I always liked it."

"Do you have a ghost story for me? About everyone else does."

"Nah," Melissa answered. "Not me. I'm too scared. I've only seen it from a distance to be honest. I've lived here all my life but I've never even been inside. Now, my husband, he's been on the porch, but he don't believe in those things. He's not from here. We met in college. I guess we're kind of boring."

"That's okay," Taryn laughed. "It's actually kind of refreshing, to tell you the truth."

"About my Donald, I can't tell you much more than what you probably already know. He was supposed to go out and feed the horses. It was right before supper. He kissed his mother, which was a little unusual, but he was said to be a thoughtful son anyway, and he went out. When he didn't come back in for supper, his father went out looking for him. He couldn't find him. Then he didn't come back in for bedtime. His brothers went out and helped look. They looked all night. Some neighbors were called and they looked for the next two days. They even looked over at Windwood Farm. Looked everywhere. Nothing. He was never seen again. His father, that would be my great grandfather, died about a year later. Supposedly from a heart attack but everyone assumed it was from a broken heart, which I guess he did really. My great grandmother died a month later, same thing. My grandmother was ten at the time."

"That's so sad."

"Yeah, just part of my family history. Of course, I'm a little cynical. After watching a lot of crime shows and Lifetime I figure he could have taken off. Met up with someone and gone up to Ohio or out west somewhere and just started over someplace new."

"Do you really think that?" Taryn asked.

"Why not?" Melissa shrugged. "It's possible. I mean, I love my family and my kids. And, I can't believe I'm even saying this to you since I don't even know you, but there are days when don't think I don't daydream about walking off into the sunset. Just think about how life must have been back then, before machinery replaced all that manual labor. Life on the farm was hard. And who knows, maybe he was having an affair with someone around here. Maybe there was someone on the side. Maybe he was writing letters to someone and nobody knew about it. I'd like to think about the bright side of things. Better than thinking about a drifter killing him or being sold to the gypsies."

"When I was little, my parents always threatened to sell me to the gypsies."

Melissa laughed. "Mine too! I thought that was a real thing."

"It probably was!"

"He was supposed to start college that winter. Or maybe it was the following summer. Anyhow, he'd been accepted. They didn't have a lot of money, though, and he was working to earn more before he went. That's how come he was still around here. Maybe if he hadn't done that and had gone on when he was supposed to, he wouldn't have disappeared."

It had been a productive weekend and she'd eaten better than she had in weeks. Between the lunch she'd scored at the Stokes County Historical Society and the supper she'd more or less invited herself to at Melissa's house, she figured she'd gained a good three pounds. That was good while it lasted. In addition to the headache she had now she'd developed a bout of nausea that kind of killed her appetite and she hadn't been eating much. She was chalking it up to all the fast food she was consuming, but if she ever made it home for more than a few days, she really needed to go in for a checkup. She would Google it all but since all roads led to cancer that was just a direction she didn't want to head down.

Today was the day she was devoting to the missing section and she was far more excited than the day probably called for. She'd worked on it a little bit the night before and done some sketches in the hotel room after going for a swim in the pool and she felt alert and refreshed. The combination of the good food and much needed companionship and conversation helped reinvigorate her.

Feeling empowered as she breezed through the front door this time, she held her camera up in front of her and sang out into the living room, "Okay guys, things are going to change around here!" It was completely quiet. Indeed, she thought she thought she heard birds singing outside. Nodding her head in approval, she did a little bit of a two-step shuffle, and bobbed her head. Skipping a little bit, she headed back to the kitchen and aimed her camera. "I'm working on the part of the house that's gone today, and I need some interior shots of the house to help me along. Anyone got a problem with that?" Again, total silence.

"Yeah," she sang. "That's what I'm talking about."

Satisfied she'd gotten the best shots possible, she skirted back to the living room and then took the camera from around her neck and turned it on playback. And stopped dead in her tracks. Where there should have been empty rooms, she saw the faint outlines of pictures, tables, and chairs. "Well, here we go again."

Then, she had an idea.

"What else can you pick up for me, Dixie?"

Ignoring the slight chill that was starting to fill the air, Taryn slung the camera back over her neck and began snapping pictures of every corner of each room she encountered. She paid little notice to where she aimed the camera and to artistic integrity, she just pointed and shot and did it as quickly as she could, before things got bad. She knew she might not have much time. The air around her thickened and turned tense but she kept moving, moving; her heart rate accelerating. She didn't take time to look at her screen, she didn't even look through her viewfinder, she just kept her eyes straight ahead as she walked from one room to the next first on the ground floor and then up one set of stairs to the master bedroom, devoid of any furniture, and the other set of stairs to Clara's bedroom.

By the time she made it back outside, the air inside the house dropped several degrees and she was shivering from the cold, despite the fact the temperature outside was close to ninety.

144

Her heart was racing from the adrenalin and she felt as though she had been walking through molasses. But she made it and nothing had flown at her, shouted at her, or cried. That was an improvement, at least.

With shaking hands, she jumped in her car and sped off toward the hotel, anxious to look at the pictures on her computer. It wouldn't do to see them on her camera. She needed to see them in the largest size possible. Certain that she'd wreck along the way or that something crazy would happen— like her camera would grow wings and fly out the window or something—she was shocked when her car arrived at the hotel in one piece.

With trembling hands, she stuck the memory card in her adapter and waited with nervous anticipation as the images loaded. She couldn't believe her eyes at what she was looking at. "Holy mother of God," she whispered.


"Good grief!" Matt shouted into the phone.

She hadn't been able to keep it to herself, of course. She'd sent them to his Dropbox right away. Now, they were looking at them together.

"I'm about to fall over, Matt. I mean, what the hell is this? Am I going out of my ever-loving mind?" Taryn paced back and forth across her hotel room, periodically going back to stare at her computer screen again, just to make sure she wasn't dreaming.

The downstairs pictures were crazy enough: the chairs in the living room, the settee in the parlor, the bookshelf filled with

145

what could only be leather-bound volumes, the area rug, the shoes waiting for someone to come back and slip them on at the bottom of the staircase...They looked like stills from a movie. These weren't faded images or holograms. Yes, there were some images that were a little blurry, as though they might be double exposures, but many of them were as strong as though the articles in question had actually been there when the pictures were, in fact, taken. Most people wouldn't doubt that they were.

It was the pictures taken upstairs, specifically the ones in Clara's bedroom, that raised the most questions. There were seven in total and six of them were similar to the ones taken downstairs. They showed a bedroom much like the one that could be seen today; the only difference being the addition of a full-length standalone mirror next to the bed that had since disappeared. But in the last image, an image Taryn could not take her eyes away from, in the center of the tousled bed, amidst the blankets and pillows in what looked like a heap of sadness and torment was the unmistakable outline of a stunning young girl.

Her figure wasn't as strong as the rest of the images. It was fragile, as if touching her might make her disappear. Parts of her were transparent, and that was disturbing enough. But the shape of her body and the sagging of her shoulders conveyed the grief Taryn heard from her cries and seeing it somehow made it even worse.

"Oh, Matt, that's her. Just seeing it, you have no idea. That's Clara, that's her. Now I've captured a ghost on film. I've gone and done it."

146

"It's a sign, Taryn. It's a sign you're supposed to finish it. She obviously needs your help. Look at the poor thing. Maybe it's about finishing your painting. Maybe that's all you need to do."

Taryn snorted. "Riiight. Because this ghost cares about oils. Clearly."

"I don't know. Maybe it has something to do with the mirror. It's the only thing missing from the room. When mirrors are facing one another, it's supposed to open the door to the spirit world. Why is that one in her room gone? Where did it go?"

Taryn rubbed her temples. "I don't know, Matt. I'm not the ghost whisperer."

"Dear, you are now, apparently."

# Chapter 8

"Well, of course Mama thinks that the old loon on Windwood Farm had something to do with that boy's disappearance," Tammy confided.

The diner was deserted and Tammy was helping herself to a scoop of ice cream, her feet propped up on a chair she had dragged over to the booth. It was late and she was pulling a double shift. The jukebox was playing early Randy Travis and Taryn couldn't sleep. She was staring at her waffles and sliding the butter around and around them, dipping it down into the little holes and back out again.

"Sounds about right, doesn't it?" she murmured.

"Sure, why not?" she agreed. Her perky ponytail bobbed on her head. She might have worked all day, but she looked fresh as a daisy. Taryn, on the other hand, felt as though she'd been dragged through the mud. Her head was pounding, her skin was oily, and she couldn't stop going to the bathroom. She must have eaten something bad.

"What's the motive though?"

Tammy shrugged, scraping the side of the ice cream dish. "I dunno. Meanness. This ain't a crime show. Sometimes folks don't need a motive. Maybe he was just mean and wanted to kill someone and that kid was in the wrong place at the wrong time."

"Sorry, be right back," Taryn apologized and jumped up and headed for the bathroom.

When she returned, Tammy was still sitting in the booth. "You okay?"

"Yeah, sorry about that. I made myself some sweet tea in the hotel room this morning and took it with me when I went to the house to work. Either it went bad, or it was something in my sandwich. My stomach's been off all day. I could be coming down with something, too. I've had a headache for over a week."

"Could be the heat. You outside every day, you've got to feel it the most," Tammy said sympathetically. "I don't know how you stand it. The best thing about this job is that it's air-conditioned in here. That and the music. I rigged the jukebox so that it plays for free. Well, and I can eat. I looove to eat."

"So did your mom have anything else to say about it?" Taryn was desperate for more information and would take anything she could get. She hadn't had any more experiences at the house since she took the pictures inside and saw whom she could only assume to be Clara in the bed. She visited her grave that morning and hoped to feel something but hadn't heard a peep or felt a thing. It had actually been peaceful and even enjoyable to visit the headstone, especially since it was now cleaned off. Of course, now that she wanted to pick up on something she couldn't. It apparently didn't work that way.

"Just that she thought you were nuts for going out there every day and that she thought they just ought to tear the damn thing down be done with it. She thinks the house is evil. She and Dad used to go out there and make out, and probably screw around, when they were dating in high school, and she saw all

149

kinds of shit. I'm not naïve. She said she heard screaming, saw black shapes flying around, heard crying. I don't know. One time she heard a man yelling 'help me' and then heard someone shoot an old timey shot gun. It was right near the car and she could smell gun smoke. They thought it was real at first but there was nobody there. That was good enough for them, though. They never went back."

"Houses like that, though, usually those are the kinds of places kids would go to and hang out at. You'd *want* to see things. I grew up outside of Nashville for the most part and there were 'haunted' houses around. Everyone wanted to see them," Taryn mused. "It was fun to be scared."

"But don't you feel like this one is different?" Tammy asked. "It's not just scary. It's sad. I don't feel good there. Being scared is fun. I love horror movies. Me and my boyfriend, we go to scary movies and I cover my eyes and scream and watch through my fingers. He makes fun of me, but I love them! And we go through haunted houses at Halloween. But it's fun! This is not fun. That house is not fun. It makes me want to cry. YouknowwhatImean?"

She said it all in a rush, like one big word. And Taryn knew exactly what she meant. Windwood Farm was more than a simply horrifically spooky place, it was crushing. And as she drove back to the hotel and parked her car under the flashing vacancy light, she finally knew that she *needed* to figure out what was going on. It wasn't because the ghost was asking her to, like in a movie. It wasn't because it was a pressing mystery that demanded to be

150

solved. It was because the sadness was so overwhelming that it might have gotten inside of her and was making her ill. She was convinced that's how much of an effect the house was having on her.

She meant to get an even earlier start than usual the next morning, but the overcast morning erupted into a strong thunderstorm and it didn't let up until after three o'clock. That ended up being just fine with her because her upset stomach never really did ease up and she was violently ill all morning from both ends until she collapsed in bed and fell into a fitful sleep until early evening.

With nothing in her room but a package of crackers and a jar of peanut butter, she made herself a snack and watched episodes of "Boy Meets World" while she dealt with her fragile tummy and moaned into her pillow. Where in the world had she picked something up? She considered painting in her room, as she didn't really need to see the house after all, but she didn't trust herself to sit up for very long.

Finally, she gave up and went back to bed where she slept through most of the night. Her underwear lay in a crumbled heap on the floor. They were just slowing her down anyway. She hoped there weren't any embarrassing streaks on her sheets for her maid to deal with. She was sure she was throwing up stuff she'd eaten weeks before. Her vomit was pure stomach acid at this point. In fact, she thought at one point she might have even thrown up

Tammy's ice cream. It was that awful. The worst part was definitely the cramps. They finally died down but during the reigning terror of hell that happened around 6:00 am, she would have happily thrown herself into the reigning arms of whatever deity presided over the afterlife just to have done away with them.

She thought she might have even called out to her mother, something she hadn't done since she was a very little girl—fat lot of good that had done her then. And then felt instantly sorry for herself and that made her cry.

Now she felt fragile but a little better. The thunder and lightning had stopped but there was still a drizzle. She didn't feel like painting or drawing, so she consoled herself by playing around on the internet. It didn't tell her much in the way of ghost photography. Many people over the years had taken pictures of what they thought were ghosts in houses, but most of these looked like, to her anyway, overexposures or tricks of the light. There was one creepy baby picture of a little one by a grave and she couldn't take her eyes off of it but nothing resembled the shots taken with her own camera and the furniture.

On a hunch, she tried Googling "Donald Adkins" and tried searching through the 1920s throughout Kentucky and the surrounding states. Maybe, just maybe, if he had up and left the county and settled somewhere nearby he hadn't changed his name and just gone somewhere else and hoped nobody noticed. But no searchable death records or marriage records showed anyone with the name marrying or dying anywhere close. It was a long shot, but it was all she had. More than likely, if he wanted to disappear he would have changed his name. Even in the 1920s, people could still be found.

Donald had simply vanished like a ghost.

Clara was dead and Donald was gone and the connection between the two was too obvious. At least to her it was. Had Donald known something he shouldn't have? Witnessed something? Had a hand in killing Clara? (She still wasn't buying the TB cause of death.) Was she completely out in left field here? So maybe it wasn't so much of a mystery, after all. Maybe she was focusing too much on the "what" when she should have been focusing on the "why."

Giving up for the night, she took the last Phenergan she had left over from the last time she had the flu and propped herself back up in bed. It wasn't that late, but she was tired and maybe one more night's sleep would make her feel better. It couldn't make her feel any worse.

The next day didn't prove to be any better, at least not weather-wise, but at least her stomach was on the mend. She decided not to take any chances on food, but did drive through Starbucks and got herself a latte. A girl had to have something to start her morning, or afternoon as it may be, off right.

Vidalia's library was in the middle of Main Street, a squat, yellowed stone building with a parking lot only large enough for ten cars (or seven pickup trucks, as it happened to be this morning). It consisted of one fairly large room with a line of

153

computers along the back wall which boasted a couple of middle aged men and women who all seemed to be checking their Facebook status updates or playing Candy Crush. A few toddlers played in the children's section with Curious George books while bored soccer mom-looking mothers played on their phones. She had seen this same scene in countless other libraries. It's funny how some things just did not change. Still, the air conditioning was refreshing and the rocking chairs by the front door were a nice touch. An elderly couple occupied them and both were engrossed in new releases and barely acknowledged her when she walked in.

"Hi, I'm from out of town and I was looking for some information on the history of the county, from about the 1920s to around the end of the Depression," she said brightly to the clerk at the desk.

The skinny sixty-something with a surprisingly hefty midsection and a shocking amount of black wavy hair and jowls that would rival Elvis' gave a large sigh. She was sure it went against the library's noise policy but he hefted himself off his stool and nobody seemed to notice. She was almost positive he rolled his eyes, although the *People* magazine he was reading was at least three months old and couldn't have been that interesting. The couple on the cover, after all, had broken up and gotten back together at least twice since that issue.

"You'll never find what you're looking for unless I show you," he complained as he marched her to the back of the room.

"Thank you," she said sweetly.

The only other people in the library, other than the couple up front, were the mothers in the children's section and a few at the computers. But he was clearly overworked and she *must* have been a burden to him...

There weren't many books to look at. One was a census report. The other was a book of photographs that the Historical Society released. That one ought to be interesting. The third was a biographical sketch about the town in general and focused in on several of the founding families. A quick glance through it showed that young Donald's family, along with the Fitzgeralds, were the primary settlers back in the early 1800s. She figured she'd start with that one, since it appeared to be the most inclusive of the bunch.

For the next four hours, she pored over the books, taking notes when she found something of interest, stopping for tea (she'd sneaked in a thermos of it and kept it hidden under her chair) and bathroom breaks when she absolutely had to. Luckily, her stomach wasn't bothering her as much as she feared it would, although it was still upset. For a county she didn't know much about and didn't have any ties to, Stokes County was far more interesting than she thought.

The original fort was constructed on the river. The Fitzgeralds and Adkins were the founding fathers and owned the most acreage at the time, each with around one thousand acres. They sold a lot of their acreage off, and gave some of it away to build the current town of Vidalia. (The current county seat, she learned, was not in its original location and had actually been moved twice.) The Fitzgeralds eventually turned to the railroad and went on to become prosperous and invested in a neighboring town on the other side of the county. It became known as Fitz, fittingly enough. Other communities popped up throughout the county with names such as Fitz Mountain and Gerald. They obviously left their mark.

The Adkins also did quite well, only they went in the way of tobacco. Kentucky soil was quite good for tobacco and they experienced several good seasons. They ended up with around 500 acres. Then, around 1919, they sold off 150 acres to a farm on the other side of them. It was a name she hadn't encountered anywhere else, but it wasn't Windwood Farm. This was a Jenkins.

The Bowens of Windwood Farm did crop up throughout the history of the county, but only as footnotes from time to time. They didn't seem to have any historical significance, other than the fact that one of the descendants did go on to become governor, although that particular one did not ever actually live in Stokes County. Much was referred to about the house, especially since the architect designed the governor's mansion and the state capitol building.

Mention was made when Leticia passed away in 1917 from TB and again when Clara passed in 1921. Very little was said about Robert's death later in 1933. She did find it interesting, however, that mention was made of Clara's "suitor," a Jonathan Fitzgerald. A quick flip back through the census showed her that he was one of the sons from the neighboring Fitzgerald farm, but at the last census, would have been fifteen years her senior. Sure, things were different then, but that was a little old for Clara, surely? Did Daddy know about that one?

In the biographical book of Stokes County, her question was answered for her. Old Jonathan Fitzgerald was a looker. In fact, posing with his two older brothers and father, and if they were any indication of how he would look when he was even older then Clara had nothing to worry about; no wonder she went for the older men. With his skinny moustache and little hat and big smile, he was all right. For the time, anyway. Besides, even a fifteen years age difference only made him, what, thirty-one? It might have been all right. Still, what was a wealthy Fitzgerald with all of his railroad money doing with a kid from a family that didn't have much but a nice house?

"That still doesn't explain Donald," she sighed. "Unless there was some kind of lover's spat and one killed the other over Clara and Robert had nothing to do with it. But it says here that Jonathan married, had seven kids, and lived to be ninety-seven."

She wasn't any closer than she was when she started.

She was tempted to put the books back on the shelf so as not to give the obviously overworked librarian any more work than he needed, but she remembered the childhood rule about always putting the books back on the little cart or leaving them on the table so she stacked them up neatly in front of her and left, noting that the old couple in the rocking chairs was gone and she was alone in the small library. Even the sniveling librarian was gone, replaced by an overweight woman who had bright orange hair and black roots and was wearing a shiny polyester top. She was reading a Nora Roberts book and sipping something from an extremely large plastic cup behind the desk. She didn't notice Taryn leave.

The bright sunshine hit her when she stepped out the door and it took her a moment to adjust her eyes. She had to almost feel her way to her car, which is why she thought she was seeing things when she first noticed her back tire. "Holy shit!" she screamed, dropping to her knees and running her hand along the frayed rubber.

It was no heat mirage, though. Not only was the right rear tire completely flat, it looked like someone had taken something very, very sharp and filleted it. They hadn't just punctured it; they had nearly sawed it right in half. "Oh my God," she seethed, to nobody in particular. "What the fuck did they do? Sit here and wait for the air to go out and then saw it in two?" And that's exactly what it looked like they had done.

Seconds later, Taryn felt the stickiness under her and realized that when she dropped to her knees she landed in a puddle of oil. At first she thought her car was leaking, another problem she'd have to get fixed, but a glance around showed her an empty bottle and in horror she saw that it was intentional: whoever murdered her tire also left this little joy for her to find as well—her own little personal swimming pool to land in. Nice.

# Chapter 9

When the police finally came, they found her stomping around the parking lot, rainbows of slimy juice running down her legs and landing in droplets on the pavement as she waved her hands and muttered to herself. She didn't resist as a nice young officer helpfully dried her off with a towel that an elderly woman from a house next door had brought over. She barely put up a fight as he helped her into the cruiser and drove her the two blocks to the station so that she could file a report.

When they started asking her who she thought might have done this, however, she went a little berserk.

"How the hell am I supposed to know?" she shrieked. "I'm not even *from* here! I don't know anyone! The only people I've met are Reagan, the property guy, the mean librarian, and the old people from the Stokes County Historical Society. So unless you want to pin it on one of them..."

"It's probably just some kid playing a prank," the better-looking of the two policemen offered helpfully. "We'll look into it."

"Don't you have some kind of surveillance video?" she asked. She knew she was pouting but she couldn't help it. Her legs burned from the oil and she was tired. And now her stomach was acting up again, but she was too embarrassed to tell the two police officers that she had diarrhea.

At her question, both men busted out laughing. The older cop, the one with a beer gut and what she only imagined was a toupee, actually doubled over. "At the library? What are they going to steal?"

"You know...books?" She answered lamely.

While she let them have their laugh, her stomach rumbled even more. Soon, she realized her stomach wasn't going to be able to be ignored any longer. "Um, guys, could I have a bathroom or something? Because—" the words weren't even out of her mouth when suddenly a gush of vomit spewed all over the table in front of her and ran down the side of the wall. She didn't have time to feel embarrassed because no sooner had she stopped throwing up than she felt her eyes roll back in her head and she was toppling to the ground before either man could reach her.


"**W**here the hell am I?" The bed was as hard as a rock and she seemed to be tied down to something. On the other hand, it was nice and cool and the drowsy feeling wasn't half bad. There was a low murmur in the air and when she opened her eyes she saw it was the TV.

"Stokes County General, sweetie," a sweet female voice answered from somewhere to the right of her. "You need anything?"

"Sure," she replied, and found that she was having trouble forming her words. "More information."

"You gave the boys a scare over at the police station. Nothing sends them running like seeing a woman fall over. You were dehydrated; pretty bad, too. Vomiting, diarrhea. Pretty sick.

They brought you over here. We got some fluids in you. You're going to be okay."

Taryn looked around and as the room came into focus, she saw that she was indeed inside a hospital room. Her window looked out into the low-rising hills and the bed next to her was empty. The nurse was busy changing her saline bag. She was short and squat with mousy brown hair, but her smile was big and she had the smoothest skin Taryn had ever seen. I've been on since five o'clock this morning. I'm getting ready to go home, but I wanted to change this. You've been beeping."

"How long have I been in here?" Taryn asked incredulously, trying to rise up on her elbows. She couldn't believe how weak she felt.

"Oh, almost twenty-four hours."

"What the fuck?" she cried, and fell back down. "I'm sorry."

"You were pretty out of it."

"What was it, the flu or something?" She couldn't believe it. She was feeling fine at the library. Well, almost fine. Better than she had been in the hotel room.

"They're calling it gastroententitis at the moment," the nurse shrugged. "It goes around sometimes. It can get pretty nasty. They sent some of your stool off to be sampled, just in case. Is your throat sore? Some of your vomit had blood in it."

"Yeah, now that you mention it. I've never had anything like that."

The nurse perched in the chair next to Taryn's bed and looked over at her, patted her leg. "Is there anyone I can call?"

161

She thought about Matt, but she knew he would just worry. At any rate, he probably already knew something was up. She didn't want him to worry any further. She'd call and let him know what happened when she was feeling better, that way he could worry all at once and be done with it.

"No, it's fine. My parents died a few years ago, and the only other family I have is an aunt in New Hampshire I haven't seen since I was a kid. I'm okay," she said dismissively.

Susan had five brothers and sisters and a grandmother whose house they still gathered at for supper every Sunday after church. She thought that sounded like one of the saddest things she'd ever heard and immediately wanted to adopt Taryn. But things were different these days and family just didn't seem to mean as much as it used to. She held her tongue and tried not to mother and cuddle the poor sick child, and she really *was* a sick one.

"Well, they're taking good care of you here, and if you need anything, just let us know. And the food's not even too bad, either. You can eat now if you want to. I'm getting off in a few minutes, but Verna's taking over, and you'll like her."

Taryn did like Verna, too. She was a grandmotherly type and she fussed over her and even brought her knitting in at one point and sat in the rocking chair in the corner. She beguiled Taryn with tales of panthers and "booger mans" that her own "nana" had told her when she was a little girl until Taryn was laughing and her sides were hurting.

Apparently, there weren't many patients in Stokes County General, at least not on her floor. When she asked, Verna laughed and waved away her concern, "Lord, no, honey. They're either old and been here for months or they're on drugs and crying for more and we can't give them anything. You're the first real sick one we've had in a long time."

"Well, not that I'm not enjoying myself, but do you think I'll get to go home tomorrow? Or at least back to my hotel?"

She was enjoying her supper of penne pasta, a homemade roll, and a tossed salad a lot more than she thought she would but she was itching to get back to work. Although she was slightly afraid to get off the Zofran through the IV. She didn't know what would happen to her stomach once she stopped taking it.

"We'll have to see what the doctor says. He'll do his rounds in the morning. They sent your labs off and you should get them back then," Verna sighed. "I tell you, the way you was carrying on, well, you looked like something out of a horror movie. I'm glad you don't remember any of it."

"Well, I remember some of it." She did remember a lot about what happened in the hotel room and that was more than enough.

Her sleep that night was as peaceful as it could be. Verna did her best to check her blood pressure and temperature without waking her up, but now that she knew she was in a hospital the night sounds kept her restless. The slamming of doors, the lights in the hallways, the rustling papers, the nurses talking at their station...she tossed and turned a lot.

At six o'clock, a Dr. Moody woke her up by clearing his throat and standing at the foot of her bed. He was several minutes into his speech before she was fully awake and listening. She was sure she missed some vital bits of information but something caught her ear and she had him go back and repeat it three times just to make sure she understood him correctly.

"Pine Sol?"

The tall, thin, blond-headed man who could have been a tennis player or PE coach nodded his head emphatically. "Yes, that's what I said. Most commonly used in household cleaning products like Pine Sol."

"Are you saying I was poisoned?

"Well, not necessarily. I'm saying that your system had ingested, in one form or another, the chemical compound—"

"So you're saying that either I drank Pine Sol myself or that someone gave it to me," she finished for him.

His cheeks turned red, making his blond hair even brighter.

"That would be the other alternative, yes."

"Do I look like the kind of person who might chug down a bottle of floor cleaner to you?" she demanded.

"Ma'am, there are high school kids out there snorting everything under the sun. I can't even begin to imagine what kinds of people may or may not do certain things," he replied apologetically.

Taryn looked down at her arm and the IV stuck in it. "Yeah, that's true I guess. But when could someone have poisoned me. And how?"

"Do you drink any tea?" Verna piped up. "Because Pine Sol looks like tea. Or coke. Same color and all. Someone could have put it in there."

"Well, I..." And sure, she did. She took tea with her when she painted. And had it with her at the library. She left it at the easel when she went inside the house, when she visited the graveside, every time she went to the bathroom...There were plenty of opportunities for someone to do something to it.

"Wouldn't you have noticed if someone had slipped something into the tea?" Dr. Moody asked.

"Not necessarily," Taryn said drily. "I make terrible tea, to start with. And since coming here, I've switched to another brand. I thought it tasted funny but chalked it up to being cheap."

None of them were able to help stifling their chuckles.

"Well, I could stand to lose a couple of pounds anyway," she muttered, feeling her flat stomach underneath her hospital gown.

"Well, frankly, you're lucky it didn't do any more damage than it did. It could have caused some serious internal bleeding. Dehydration is no joking matter, young lady. A few more days of that vomiting and diarrhea and you might have been facing some really serious damage," he lectured.

"Oh, I know," she agreed. "But I don't know who could have done this. This wasn't the work of some ghost. Long story," she waved away at the look of confusion on his face.

She agreed to remain in the hospital under observation for another twenty-four hours. She didn't mind. She still felt weak and, besides, they had more channels than the hotel's cable anyway.

After the doctor left Verna clucked her tongue. "I know you're working at Windwood Farm and I know what you mean about the ghosts. But you're dealing with a real live person here, missy."

"Yes, I know," Taryn agreed. "They slashed my tire, too. I'm sure it's the same one."

"Probably a kid, no doubt. When I was growing up and my kids were little, this was a different place. Kids today, no respect. They just don't care no more, you know what I mean? The place is a ghost town. Why, you used to be able to ride the train from here to Fitz and go shopping, get an ice cream cone, eat lunch, and then come back. Now the whole place is just about gone. Stores all boarded up. It's sad. Built a bypass around the whole town."

"What happened to the Fitzgeralds, anyway?"

"Same as everyone else, I reckon. Some went off to college and never come back. 'Brain drain', they call it. Passenger rail gone away. Lost money. Some moved up north and worked in the factories after the war. Just spread out into the wind. A few still around here. None of them have the money the old family used to. The old house ain't even still standing. Whole thing divided off and made into subdivisions: every house built of the same material and looks the same. Come home after dark and how are you supposed to know which one is yours?"

Taryn laughed.

"Do you know anything about Jonathan Fitzgerald?"

Verna nodded. "I met him once. Of course, he was an old man when I was a little girl. He lived in his daddy's house and didn't get out much. I'd see him in town sometimes. Always pretty friendly. His wife was a little strange. I was in Dickerson's, that was a general store on Main Street, once and I didn't have enough money for some candy. He bought me a handful and smiled. She snapped at him, mean-like, and he said to hush. That was the only time I met him. He dressed real fine."

"Did you know he was supposed to marry Clara Bowen from Windwood Farm?"

Verna shrugged. "I heard that, but she died so young. Of course, I never met her. I heard stories about *her* daddy, but he died before I was born too, and that house has been empty my whole life. My friends have gone out there and tried to see the ghosts. Some of them have seen and heard things, but I never messed around with it. My mama always told me that you don't do that. That you might bring something home with you if you do. And my mama didn't raise no fool."

# Chapter 10

Despite the fact the hospital staff had been compassionate and the food exceptionally good for hospital fare, Taryn was ready to break loose and get her car back. The local garage that the tow truck had hauled it to had taken pity on her and replaced the tire for free, even without her having full coverage, and then driven it over to the hotel for her. One of the nurses took her to the hotel when she got off duty and that saved her a cab fare. This was all good news since she was really starting to have bad thoughts about small central Kentucky towns in general.

Once she got the poison diagnosis, she'd had to file yet another police report. But this meant more visitors, and for a brief moment, she'd felt like a celebrity. The police had come in and seen her and done their thing (they'd interviewed everyone at the library that afternoon but nobody had seen a thing, of course), Reagan stopped by with flowers and his stunning little wife and come by and pampered her with chocolates and bubble bath from Bath and Body Works. A group of women (and the one solitary man) from the Stokes County Historical Society made a brief appearance and cooed and clucked over her, offered sincere apologizes, and even shed a couple of tears over her pale appearance. The bird-woman seemed particularly upset and brought an apple pie, which everyone assured her was the best she would ever eat. Taryn took a couple of bites while everyone watched her and was, indeed, amazed at the tartness and juiciness it offered her.

So, all in all, her hospital stay was not a bad one.

But she was ready to leave. She felt a little silly as they wheeled her down the elevator, balancing her pie, flowers, and bubble bath in her lap. But she bet she made a better picture than she did when coming in, covered in vomit and feces.

Back in her hotel room, she changed out of the sweatpants and T-shirt the hospital had given her. She'd had nothing but the soiled dress she'd been wearing at the police station, and she'd made sure they'd thrown that away since it was covered in gunk and oil, and put on her pajamas. She then went to work calling Matt and plugging in her laptop.

"Hey dude," she said into the phone as her computer booted up. "So, listen, I've had a little incident, but I'm okay."

He listened quietly as she ran through the events and told him what she knew.

"You should have called me," he finally said when she was finished. "I would have come up there."

"I know. That's why I didn't call you." She had dozens of emails, mostly job offers. She'd sort through those later. "But I feel okay now, still a little fragile, but the stuff is out of my system. The vomiting and diarrhea was good, actually, it was getting it out. And you know, the police think it was probably just some kid playing a prank on me. Trying to make me scared since I'm working at that house and all. I'm fine, really. So listen, I found out some information and I want to run it by you—"

"So that's just how it's going to be then?" he asked, his voice still quiet. "Some crazy person is going to poison you and try to kill you and I'm just going to stay down here and wait for you to call and tell me that everything is 'fine' and call me whenever you feel like it and I'm supposed to be okay with that? That's not okay, Taryn."

"I'm sorry. I didn't want you to worry, that's all. And I mean that. I'm used to taking care of myself. Look, they have a very nice hospital up here and everyone was really helpful. It's stopped raining and I can finish the damn painting now and get out of here. I'll just stop drinking tea, that's all," she joked.

Matt groaned. "It's not funny."

"I feel really, really bad, if it helps."

Matt sniffed. "It does, a little."

She did feel bad. Matt was in the same boat she was in. His family sucked in a different kind of way. He had one but they didn't care. Hers might be dead but his didn't know he was alive, which was kind of weird since he really should have been the golden child with his big brains and good job. They rarely saw each other, though, and more often than not, he spent his holidays alone except for the times when she coaxed him to visit her or she went down and stayed with him and they celebrated together. Their families were a lot alike that way, or had been when hers was alive. She would do better at keeping him updated.

"So what did you find? I'm all ears."

She spent the next hour updating him on the news, little as it was. He was nothing if not a good listener and she smiled as she heard him scribbling notes. No wonder he graduated a year in advance. When she was finished she put him on speakerphone and let him process the information while she ran herself a bubble bath, courtesy of Mrs. Jones, and sank into it while he mumbled to himself and let his brain work.

"So what I think we have ourselves here is either some kind of weird love triangle or some really off-the-wall coincidence that has nothing to do with anything. That's how I see it."

"That's what I'm seeing, too," she agreed. "Either Clara was stringing both men along and Jonathan killed Donald out of jealousy and then refused to marry her because she was 'soiled' or some shit like that or she really did die of TB before he could marry her and Donald's disappearance has nothing to do with Clara at all and he just took off."

"Do we think Clara and Jonathan were really in love? Fifteen years age difference? Wealthy man and daughter of man in debt? That's not ringing true for me..."

"I don't know either. Something seems off. But it could've happened. The only thing I know about Jonathan, other than his family and money, was that he brought sweets for a kid once, nothing seems to say he was a bad guy."

"So the one thing we know for sure is that Robert did die, probably from a heart attack, but he wasn't murdered. We know that Jonathan Fitzgerald eventually married someone else and lived happily ever after. He was never legally tainted with anything bad. We also know that although Robert died owing a lot of people money, he never lost his farm, right?"

Taryn, whose body had finally relaxed under the steam and bubbles, rose up out of the water. "Matt! That's a really, really good point. And a really obvious one. If he was in so much debt, and owed everyone so much money, how was he able to keep his house? What was he doing to earn money? We know it sold after his death, and that the farm was worked because nobody lived in the house, but I've never once asked anyone what Robert did. I just assumed he was a farmer. Was he taking out loans? Did they just keep giving them to him?"

"All good questions and a good place to start. Shouldn't be hard to figure out. I'd try to see if you could find any records. The historical society might have financial records of property taxes."

"And I do need to work, too, eventually," she sighed.

"How's that part going?"

"It's going. Some parts are easier than others. I'm going to have to make a supply run up to Lexington tomorrow. It will feel good to get out of town anyway, I think."

"Good, because there's a man I want you to stop and see. I'll tell him you're coming and he'll be waiting for you," Matt said.


Taryn had spent her time in the hospital stressing about not working on the painting, even though the folks from the Stokes County Historical Society and Reagan both told her not to worry about it. She hated falling behind, though, and the little detour had cost her nearly a week's worth of work. She wasn't sure how far her funds were going to stretch at this point and she was antsy to get back on the road.

On the other hand, a huge part of her wasn't ready to leave. She was tied to the house, hook, line and sinker, whether she liked it or not. She'd bought into the stories just like everyone else in the county apparently had, only for some reason now she felt like the house had chosen her to unravel its secrets. True, her camera only seemed to pick up on things when the house wanted to reveal them, but she felt so close to knowing the truth that she couldn't stop now if she'd wanted to.

Now that she was back in her hotel room, though, she couldn't work up the motivation to get the painting out and work on it. It rested on its easel in the corner of the room, watching her as she tried to ignore it. "I know you're there," she said in its general direction. "And I promise I'll get back to you. I have some other things right now, though, so you'll have to wait."

She was amazed at the number of online communities that targeted the paranormal and after spending a couple of hours sifting through them, reading forums and websites and even getting involved in a live chat, she felt like her head was spinning. Was everyone in the world psychic or clairvoyant or some combination? She was astonished to find there were even classes that offered certifications to help people develop their intuition and "powers." She never knew such things existed.

"I've been living under a rock," she muttered out loud.

Of course, when you spent the majority of your time studying the culture and lives of people from several centuries before, it was easy to be surprised at the flippancy and acceptance that such things were shown today. This wasn't Salem, after all. Now, being a witch was actually something most people seemed to be proud of. Indeed, they even offered classes and certifications for it.

But nothing, in all of her searching, showed her anything that came close to what she was experiencing. She read about haunted houses and mediums and those who could converse with the dead (some people had their own reality shows), and some of these people even sounded like they might be legitimate, but she didn't find anything that had to do with taking photographs of the past. Of course, she'd already been down that road and had come up empty handed before, but she figured it didn't hurt to try again.

After visiting one forum where the members chatted about developing their intuition and sensitivities, she sat back and blew out some air she'd been holding in. "These are my people," she laughed. "Is this what I'm really in for?" She didn't think she'd be handing over money any time soon but reading about the process was fascinating.

The man Matt wanted her to see was the owner of a store called "New Age Gifts and More." The "and more" included small appliance repair. The shop was located in a strip mall and situated between a Showbiz Pizza and a Habitat for Humanity Restore. It was bright and cheery and she was immediately greeted by the scent of incense and candles. One side was lined with crystals balls, Tarot cards, essential oils, candles, and gemstones. The other side had televisions, laptops, PS4s, and iPhones behind display cases. It was a little surreal but the store clerk at the end of the store had a big smile and threw up a big wave at her as she took a few steps forward. He wore a Hank Williams T-shirt (Sr., not Jr.) and was reading a biography on the Dalai Lama.

"Can I help you with anything?"

"I'm not sure, really," she stammered. "My friend sent me here. I don't know what I'm looking for."

"Are you...Taryn?"

"Yes, that's me!" she said brightly.

"Ah ha! I thought I'd recognize you. He said you'd have long, red curly hair and be knock-down gorgeous and here you are. Frankly, we don't get many of those around here."

"Matt flatters me, I'm afraid."

"Nah," he laughed. "All true. But I have what you need. He says you're having trouble with some vision and you also need a little bit of protection."

"Protection maybe, but I don't want to stop seeing things," she hedged.

"Of course not," he agreed, his eyes twinkling behind his black curly beard. "But that doesn't mean you don't need a little help."

"So you don't think I'm crazy?"

"Hell, no. Are you nuts? I'd give anything to do what you're doing. Don't worry, your secret's safe with me," he said hurriedly at her protest. "I don't have much of the sight myself, and nothing like what our friend Matt described is going on with you."

"I studied Historical Preservation in college and to tell you the truth, this is a little bit of a dream come true for me," she confided to this total stranger, happy to have someone new to share her secret with, someone who appeared to take her at face value. "To see the past as it once was, well, I guess that's the dream for someone like me, right?"

"I get you, I get you. I love old buildings, ruins, abandoned places. Me and my girlfriend, we're urban explorers, you know what I mean?"

She nodded her head. "Break into old houses and stuff, walk around, take pictures?"

"Right on! We love to check out things from the past, imagine what it used to look like. Don't get me wrong, I love modern technology. I have three TVs and an iPhone, you know what I mean? But give me an old farmhouse over a subdivision any day."

"Me too. When I was a kid and the teacher asked us all what we wanted to be when we grew up, everyone else said doctors, lawyers, teachers...I said I wanted to be a time traveler. Joke's on me, right?" she smiled.

They laughed.

"Doesn't it freak you out, though?" he asked. "Matt, he's real worried about you. Said someone tried to kill you. That's not a ghost, you know."

"No, that's a person. And I have no idea who's doing it. And yeah, I'm scared. A lot. But mostly I'm curious. The noises, the scents, the sounds...But when I'm looking through the camera and seeing the pictures, it's like watching a movie, like viewing it through another time period. Like I'm not really there."

"So you're kind of detached from the scene."

Taryn felt herself grow slightly uncomfortable at the thought, but couldn't understand why. "Yeah, maybe."

"Well," he said, bringing a paper bag up from behind the counter and handing it to her. "Here are some things that will get you started. Some sage for your hotel room and car. That will cleanse them, purify them, get rid of any bad mojo you got hanging around. A pentagram to wear around your neck, I blessed it myself. Some black candles to light in your room to help ward off negative energy..."

By the time she left the shop, she'd spent $75, had more New Age paraphernalia than she knew what to do with, and was the proud owner of a new 22-inch flat screen television.


Lexington was a nice town. She treated herself to the Fayette Mall where she shopped at Macy's and bought herself some new boots and spent several lovely hours people watching and then went to the movies and laughed at a silly comedy that she promptly forgot. The countryside with its horse farms and ornate mansions were intermixed with an eclectic, hip downtown area filled with Victorian houses and urban restaurants with outdoor seating

177

areas. She thought she could spend time in a town like this, she found herself thinking on more than one occasion, especially when she was settled at the enormous bookstore, sipping on a mocha and relaxing in an overstuffed chair.

It was good to get away from Vidalia and Windwood Farm where she was starting to feel a little stuffy and even paranoid. After all, someone had tried to make her very sick, if not altogether dead. She actually liked small towns and figured she'd settle down in one sooner or later, but so far, what with ghosts keeping her from her work, surly librarians, and poisons being tossed into her tea, this one wasn't exactly rolling out the welcome mat. Although the hospital *had* been very nice and she had built a good rapport with the diner waitress and Donald's descendent.

Soon, it was time to pack it in and head home. She stopped at the artists' supply store on the way back to the interstate and picked up what she needed and waved a fond farewell to the glimmering lights of the city before heading south. She'd get started again first thing in the morning. It wouldn't take her much longer to finish the painting now.

**B**ack in the hotel room, Taryn set everything from New Age Gifts and More out on the dresser and took a good look at it all. She had no idea where to start. One was a book entitled "Candle Magic" and the clerk had helpfully dog-eared and highlighted a page entitled "gaining vision and clarity on a situation." Well, she guessed she needed it, although she wasn't sure if it was in regards as to who poisoned her or what was going on in the house. Either way, clarity would be nice.

There were an awful lot of candles involved in this ritual. She hoped she wouldn't burn down the hotel room with them or set off the smoke alarm. That would be bad. She felt kind of silly setting them up: seven white ones and seven light blue ones. She lined them up, little votive candles, in two rows on the dresser. Before she lit them, she turned off her lights and then knelt down in front of the dresser. It would have to do as her altar, since she had nothing else. Matt made sure she had a big thick white candle to work as her "altar candle." She lit it first and then lit the sage incense she'd been given.

Next, she rubbed the carnation oil from all the candles' wicks to their ends and then lit them, one by one. In front of the row of candles, she placed three stones: a chrysoprase, geode, and tiger's eye. (She thought the tiger's eye sounded prettier, but it was kind of a dull stone in comparison to the geode.)

Lastly, she closed her eyes and said the chant the clerk told her to say. That was the worst part about it. Honestly, she believed in this stuff. It was one of the reasons why she and Matt continued to have the bond they did. Neither one ascribed to any kind of organized religion, although she did sometimes attend church services, but she did like the idea of an earthy kind of religion that looked to nature. But saying chants with rhyming words sounded Dr. Seuss to her, and not in a good way. It felt silly.

Still, if it helped...

She tried to clear her mind and imagine her heart free and open to clarity and truth. It was hard. Meditating was always hard. Just as soon as she told her mind to clear, it wanted to fill with every single commercial jingle or holiday song it had ever heard. It was particularly fond of the Muppets' version of "The 12 Days of Christmas."

Finally, when she felt like she had given it enough time, she opened her eyes, blew out her altar candle, and turned on the lights. The votive candles she would leave to burn out through the night and would then dispose of the wax the next morning. She wasn't quite sure what was supposed to happen next. Would it come through a dream? A phone call? A billboard?

Oh well, she thought, as she drifted off to sleep, the flickering candles making crazy patterns on the ceiling and walls. At least she tried.

# Chapter 11

Since someone had slit her tire and tried to kill her, Tammy refused to let her pay for her breakfast anymore. She insisted that her manager agreed that all future meals were to be on the house and Taryn was no fool. She didn't argue. She did, however, tip very well.

"Are you sure you don't need anything else?" she asked Taryn with real concern. "I'd offer you tea, but…"

"It's fine," Taryn laughed. "My taste for tea kind of comes and goes right now. I'm good with the water."

She was able to joke around about her hospitalization and tried to go along with the police's theory that it had just been a vicious prank, but inside she was scared. She knew she'd been poisoned more than once and that was no joking matter. Reagan offered to send some men over to stay with her while she was painting, but she had waved him away. The last thing she needed was a bunch of people all up in her business. Besides, she could usually get at least one bar on her cell phone while she was out there, despite the fact it was supposed to be a "dead zone" and Melissa was less than a mile away. She was going to finish this job, crazy people and ghosts be damned.

"Nothing like that has ever happened before, not around here anyway," Tammy said. "I mean, we've had people kill other people, but it's mostly been when they were drinking or something. Sometimes drugs. Always a knife or a gun. I've never heard of anyone trying to poison somebody."

"And I just thought I made bad tea," Taryn smiled as she drank down the last of the water. "Really, though, I'm fine."

She was about to get up and start the early morning paint session when a soft voice carried across the room and called out her name. "There's our star artist!"

Taryn turned around and saw Phyllis, the bird-woman, seated in a corner booth with a middle-aged man in suspenders and a baseball cap.

"Hello there," she waved. The man flashed her a quick smile and then went back to his biscuits and gravy.

"How are you feeling, sweetie?" she asked with what appeared to be genuine concern. "You still look a little pale yet."

"I'm feeling a lot better," she replied honestly. "I have my appetite back. They said that's good."

"Just awful," Phyllis shook her head in disgust. "And so embarrassing for our town, too. This is my son, Roger, by the way. He lives over in Fitz and takes me to breakfast once a week."

Taryn said hello and then excused herself from the diner. It hadn't escaped her attention that the other patrons were holding on to every word in the exchange. Between that and the write up in the local paper, everyone really was going to know what had happened to Vidalia's newest resident.

With her easel under her arm, Taryn set up with a new resolution. Nothing was going to stop her today. She was ready. Miss Dixie was ready too, armed and ready with a fully-charged battery. Taryn took a few test shots of the house and looked at them in the LCD screen. Nothing but decay and ruin. Well, clarity wasn't coming yet. Maybe the poison had weakened her sight. Maybe it was something she couldn't control...yet, anyway.

It didn't matter right now. She did have a job to do, after all.

And do it, she did.

For the next several hours, Taryn was a whirlwind of oil and color, painting with a ferocity that sometimes surprised those around her who didn't know her well. It probably would have been easy for someone to have come up and slipped something into her tea, but this time she wasn't taking any chances—she brought Ale-8s, the locally-produced caffeinated drinks, and they had pop caps on them.

Nearly four hours had gone by before she stopped and took a break. She was covered in sweat and grime and specks of paint, but she felt good. It was almost completed. Another day and it just might be. And then she could do some touch-ups and present it to both Reagan and the Stokes County Historical Society and be on her way. Except, of course, she couldn't really be.

It wasn't over yet.

With a sigh of frustration, she put down her paintbrush and picked up Miss Dixie again and aimed her at the house. "Oh, come on," she complained. "Give me something I can work with. How am I supposed to help you if you don't give me *something*?"

Barely paying attention at where she was pointing the camera, she aimed it at the general direction of Clara's window and took a shot. When she turned it back around and looked through the LCD screen, the faint outline of a woman stood there, looking out into the yard. "Hot damn!" Taryn hollered. "Stay there, stay there, stay there," she chanted as she took off into the house.

Sprinting toward the front door it occurred to her that it would be ironic if it were the camera that was the one with the "sight" and not her after all. But then, that would have been ignoring all of the other experiences she'd had in her life-experiences she'd tried to push away and forget. Maybe the camera was just the conduit.

"I can't rush it," she breathed quietly. "Stay calm."

She began on the first floor again, this time starting with the living room. Standing in the middle of the floor, she turned in a slow circle and took pictures as she moved, watching the screen. Again, the room came to life with furniture and knickknacks and signs of life from the past. A few items were different in these images: a new clock here, the shoes that were in the last set of pictures were now gone, but otherwise the room remained unchanged. In the kitchen, breakfast dishes were left out on the table. Signs of bacon, eggs, jam, and biscuits could be seen. But nothing appeared out of the ordinary. The table was set for two. That told her that Clara's mother must already be gone.

The dining room was empty and bare. Fearing that she might be losing whatever power the house had, she quickened her pace and headed up the stairs, careful not to run, but aware that the energy around her was changing again, becoming crushing. *Please let it last, please let it last,* she chanted to herself. On some level, she knew that this might just be her last shot.

Propitiously, with the first shot, she saw that the past was once again alive. Although no signs of Clara were apparent this time, the wardrobe door was open, revealing a small array of cotton dresses inside. They were shorter, but not girlish. Clara was not quite a little girl then, but not as old as she was when she died. A teddy bear was placed in the middle of the bed, something Taryn found sweet and sentimental considering Clara's age, which had to be at least early teens. The mirror, now gone, was still there. Clara's own reflection didn't appear, although she was standing in front of it. *Interesting,* she thought, *so I don't show up in this time period. That means they can't see me and aren't aware of my presence then.* The keys, which were on the dresser in real life, were not on there in the past.

In disappointment, Taryn sat down on the floor and stared at the LCD screen. She had so been hoping the ritual last night would help her. Maybe those things really were just bogus P.R. Maybe she didn't take it seriously enough. But she had *tried.*

Closing her eyes, she tried in vain to think of something else she could do. What was she missing? Missing. Missing...

Missing!

The mirror was missing.

Opening her eyes, she looked back at the picture of the mirror again. From its vantage point, it had a perfect view of the dresser. Although it didn't catch her reflection in it, she herself wasn't there in the past, and it didn't show the keys, it *did* show something else—something that wasn't there in the present: a small leather-bound book.

"I know a diary when I see one," she laughed almost hysterically. "Now where the hell are you?"

She might have been afraid to open things before, but sheer adrenalin and intrigue motivated her now. She'd been a teenage girl once and while her mother hadn't been a big snoop (she hadn't cared enough), Taryn kind of hoped that she might be and had come up with some glorious hiding places. On her hands and knees, Taryn searched under the dresser, inside the wardrobe, in the trunk, and under the mattress (disturbing a family of mice). She made a bad scrape on her knee from a really big cut in the floor while searching under the bed and a trail of blood dribbled down her leg. She barely noticed it, such was her excitement.

"I know you didn't take it out of the room..."

Walking to the low window, she squatted down to peer outside and her foot slipped on a loose board that nearly came up and hit her in the head. "Shit!"

Looking down, a small bundle of cloth peeked out at her inside a hole under the floorboards. "Oh, well, there you are. The classics never really die, do they?"

It was so fragile she was almost afraid to touch it but she handled it gingerly and reverently. A quick look through it showed her that the pages were shockingly dry, considering it had been hidden under an open window for more than seventy-five years. Unfortunately, only around twenty-five of the pages were written on. The rest were empty.

"Oh, honey. I was hoping you'd given me more to work with than this," Taryn complained. "But I'll work with what I've got."

Not wanting to look a gift horse in the mouth, she took her precious cargo and camera and went back downstairs, the forgotten blood drying on her leg.

# Chapter 12

*May 21, 1921*

*Sometimes I can't even remember what my mother looked like. I slip down to the parlor and look at her portrait, but it's as though I'm seeing someone from a fairy tale or a book. I can't envision her face or bring her features to my mind anymore. I can't even remember her scent. Papa won't speak her name. He says she's with the angels now, when he speaks of her at all. He has stopped attending church, too. I go alone, when he lets me go. I barely remember the way he was when she was alive. There are days when I miss Papa even more than I miss her.*

*May 28, 1921*

*Jonathan Fitzgerald came over today and we went riding in the back field. I was surprised Papa allowed me to go alone but he encouraged me and said Jonathan is a "fine young man." He is a very nice man but he seems old—not because he is several years older than myself but because he rarely laughs and his humor is deprecating. He felt old to me even when he was the age I am now. I don't think he has ever been young. He is quiet and polite and always asks me what I am thinking and what I want to talk about, however, and that is nice. I get flustered because sometimes I just want to be quiet, and not always speak so much.*

*He and Papa talk business, mostly about the railroad. I prefer my
books and have little to add to these conversations, but they do
appear to be very happy together, and I enjoy seeing Papa
happy. It happens so rarely these days. Papa spends much of his
time angry and hostile. Nothing I do seems to please him much.*

*June 3, 1921*

*I was so lonely today. I went for a walk along the ridge alone and
I watched the sunset after dinner. Papa was in town and didn't
come home until quite late. I don't mind being alone, I do prefer it
to his heated temper and periods of agitation, but I do wish I had
someone to laugh with and talk to. On the ridge I saw the Sally
Ann Farm with its smoke and running children and horses. I
heard laughter and I wanted to run down the hillside and join
them. If only I could! Papa said Mr. Adkins is terrible with money
and is selling their farm, piece by piece, and I think perhaps we
should as well. Papa refuses, although I know we are in debt. He
says unkind things about Mr. Adkins, but I've always thought
him to be polite and Donald is a terribly sweet and sensitive
young man. We were in school together before I had to stop going
to tend to the farm full time. When we were children, we played
together as well, back when Mama was alive.*

*June 25, 1921*

*Donald Adkins came to visit Windwood Farm today. Papa was in town and Donald came to see him about a business matter. I don't know its nature, but he said he would return. We spent an hour together on the front porch, and I was surprised to learn that he had read many of the same books that I have. We used to attend the same school, but I haven't been in school for going on three years now, not since Mama died and Papa needed me here at home. Donald is going to college next year and is excited about it. To hear him speak of getting a degree is exhilarating. He is so lively, with his rosy cheeks and thick hair and sparkling eyes. Almost everything he says, he says with a laugh. On his way off the porch, he tripped and fell over the steps and instead of getting mad, he laughed and laughed and then did a little bow. If I were to attend college, I like to think I might become a teacher. Of course, we don't have the money for me to go, but I do think I would do very well at it if I could.*

*June 30, 1921*

*Papa was angry when he discovered Donald had come by. He wouldn't tell me why, but he immediately went to Sally Ann Farm and came back an hour later, even more hot-tempered and said that we wouldn't be "bothered" again. I am sorely disappointed because I very much enjoyed my brief visit from Donald and I wasn't bothered at all. Papa did say Jonathan Fitzgerald would be coming back in a few days to speak to me about something important. I am unsure as to what this could be. I have never* seen much of the Fitzgeralds before. Their house and farm are grand and they keep to social circles that do not concern us. Mama always said they thought they were better than we were, despite the fact Mama also grew up in a fine house. I don't know much about these things, although Jonathan has always been nice enough. I only met my grandparents when I was small and don't remember their house.

August 5, 1921

Jonathan Fitzgerald has asked me for my hand in marriage. This is such a shock to me because although I have known him my whole life, I really barely know him at all. He isn't old enough to be my father, but I've never thought of him in that manner, not in the kind of manner to marry him. He is handsome, as most of my friends in school thought, but as a husband! I just don't know. I told him I would have to ask Papa, but then he told me that he had already asked him himself and Papa said he'd given him his blessing. I spoke to Papa about the matter, and Papa said I should accept it. I'm confused. Papa thundered through the house, asking why I would even consider refusing such a "fine offer" from someone of "such character and wealth."

Naturally, I don't know him well enough to love him. Papa told me I could learn to love him and would get to know him. That doesn't feel the same to me, however. I always thought that when I married someone, it would be because I had fallen in love with him. I am scared to refuse him now, however, because

*Papa told me that it was "necessary" for me. I don't know what that means, but it frightened me. I told him I accepted. He seemed elated and said his parents would be as well. I don't know how, since they don't even know me. He said we could set a date of sometime in the autumn. He has family who live in the north and they will want to travel here.*

*This all feels somewhat surreal to me. I love Windwood Farm. It just feels like I am destined for something else, not living with the Fitzgeralds. I thought he was going with Maizie Casteel. I saw them together in town all the time. I'm not sure what is happening to me.*

*When he asked me to marry him, I couldn't help but think of the nice conversation I had with Donald Adkins about books. It made me sad.*

*August 10, 1921*

*There's a special spot in the woods I enjoy visiting. It isn't much, just a little clearing, but there's a tree that fell over years ago and the log has made a nice bench of sorts. I go there with my books after I've done my chores and I relax when Papa is out in the fields. I went there this afternoon and had barely been there for half an hour when who should show up but Donald Adkins. He was surprised as I was!*

*"I just discovered this a week ago," he exclaimed.*

*I told him it has been mine for years, but that I was happy to share it with him.*

192

*He brought his own books so we sat, side by side, for at least an hour and read in companionable silence. I brought my lunch with me, egg salad sandwich and an apple, and I shared this with him. He brought a thermos of buttermilk and some biscuits his mother made and he shared this with me. We barely spoke a word to one another but it was one of the nicest afternoons I've had in years. We agreed to meet there every other day at the same time. He said he always has chores, but his parents allow him to have time to read since he is preparing for college. They truly value education. I asked him not to tell anyone that we were meeting because I don't think Papa would understand. He agreed.*

*August 15, 1921*

*Jonathan took me dancing tonight in town at the ballroom. There was a band playing and it was the first time I had ever been to anything like that, except for the fair, of course. The music was fast and I didn't know any of his friends, but I had a nice time. Maizie was there and that was extremely uncomfortable. She was polite to me, but sneered at me throughout the evening whenever she thought Jonathan wasn't looking and I kept getting the feeling she was making fun of me and my flowered dress and brown shoes. They were my mother's and the fanciest shoes I own. I don't have a lot of dress-up clothes, only clothes I wear to church. The ballroom was full of women in red dresses, short dresses, and lots of makeup. I don't own any makeup because*

*Papa says painted women are the devil's work and he won't allow me to wear any. I wouldn't know how to wear it even if I did have any, but seeing the other women with it on tonight made me wish I could have at least had some color on my lips. I felt very young. Jonathan promised once we were married, he would find me clothing and a hairstyle that was more suitable to me. He said he didn't want to change me, but that he didn't want me to feel uncomfortable. I am not opposed to this and think it might even be fun. Still, I was awfully glad to come back home at the end of the evening. I thought Papa would be angry we were out so late, but he said that as long as I was with Jonathan, everything was "fine."*

*August 21, 1921*

*I am so enjoying my afternoons with Donald. Most days, we don't talk to each other at all, at least not much. I read a book he encouraged me to read by Willa Cather called* My Antonia *and it made me cry for days. I just cannot stop thinking about it. He read one of my recommendations,* The Turn of the Screw, *and it kept him up for days, so we're even, I guess.*

*When we talk, we end up laughing a lot. He makes up silly songs and we take turns finishing each other's lyrics. Sometimes they're about the same people we know. A few days ago, we made up one about Maizie Casteel and her long, pointy nose. I know that sounds mean, but she really had no reason to make me feel so uncomfortable. Jonathan told me she called off the*

194

relationship with him. I told Donald about feeling underdressed at the dance and he said he understood. He talked about how he often felt bad at school because his family doesn't have a lot of money, despite the fact they live on a large farm. He has won a scholarship for college and is saving his money by working for other farmers when he can. He is a hard worker and also very intelligent. I know his parents must be proud of him.

Yesterday, Donald and I went for a walk. It was just around the woods, but I pointed out some of the herbs that I enjoy using to brew some of my favorite teas and he showed me some bark that Indians used to use for medicines. He's very knowledgeable about these kinds of things. Later, he tripped and fell into me and I teased him about trying to play tag, as though we were children. We ended up running through the woods, laughing, chasing one another. I feel like I have a real friend, for the first time in a long time.

*August 28, 1921*

Tonight, I overheard Papa and Jonathan talking about oil. They were at the kitchen table and didn't know I could hear them. Jonathan was very excited and discussing the contract options that a company could make with him, but Papa reminded him that nobody is allowed to drill until after the wedding. This made my blood run cold. I don't understand. I could feel tears stinging my eyes, but I didn't understand why. Why can't they drill until *after the wedding? I didn't even know that we had oil on our farm.*

*September 5, 1921*

*Donald assured me that Papa probably doesn't want any drilling done until after the wedding because there is a lot going on. We have set the date for December 14th and that isn't too far away. Maybe he is right. There is a lot of planning underway. I've been to town three times to have my dress sized and I've already been to the Fitzgerald farm once to have tea with Jonathan's mother, a stern woman who rarely cracks a smile. I think she would prefer he be marrying Maizie. I also met Jonathan's sister. She has even less humor than her brother.*

*Donald did confide in me that the business he sought with my Papa that afternoon was a financial one. Papa owed Mr. Adkins money and was meant to repay it that day. He still hasn't repaid the loan. Donald says the word about town is that he owes money to a lot of people, so maybe if there is an oil well on our land that is a good thing. Perhaps Jonathan is helping him in find a company to drill, then that will solve our financial debts. I do hope so. I couldn't bear to lose our farm. This is my home.*

*September 10, 1921*

*There were many things I hoped to accomplish today, but it was all I could do to stay around the house and finish the chores. My* stomach has felt funny for a few days. I've been hungry and having what feels like hunger pains, and my stomach is certainly grumbling enough, but I find when I eat I'm unable to get much down. I suppose it's just nerves. I do hope they pass soon.

September 15, 1921

These are the last few warm days of summer. Today Donald and I slipped off to the creek and cooled down in the water. It was blazing hot, so I brought my swimsuit and we splashed around like children, dunking each other in and holding each other down until we couldn't take it anymore. We laughed and laughed and then lay on the banks and watched the clouds, talking about his future plans.

"I'll miss you when you're gone, you know," I told him wistfully.

"You'll be an old married woman, you won't have time," he said playfully.

I'm not sure why, but I burst into tears and he put his arms around me while I just cried and cried and cried. When I stopped I realized I had completely embarrassed myself and I quickly dried off and got dressed. I went on home then because I just couldn't stand for him to feel sorry for me.

*September 30, 1921*

*Jonathan took me to town for lunch today. He wanted to surprise me by letting me pick out something for our new parlor. Although we'll be living in his parents' home for a time, we will have our own parlor. I have never picked out any furniture before and, having no idea what to look for, I chose a lamp since I love to read. He laughed at my choice but then gave me a hug and said he honestly did cherish me and love me. I think he might have meant it.*

*We ran into Maizie while we were in town and she commented on how "pale" I looked and said I needed to spend more time in the sun. I actually felt rather well today and assumed she was just trying to cause trouble. Jonathan told me I looked beautiful. When I got home, however, I looked in my mirror and I did appear a little peaked. Perhaps I should get out in the sun more while the weather is still nice. I can already feel the tips of winter trying to sneak in and steal the last drops of summer and I'm not ready to let them go. My hands are cold and I can't seem to get warm anymore.*

*October 15, 1921*

*I finally felt well enough to face Donald again. My stomach has been in knots and I've even been a little nauseated, but I wanted to see him and apologize. He had been showing up at our spot every day, patiently waiting for me. As soon as I started talking to him, though, he grabbed me by the shoulders and shushed me.*

*"Please don't do that, Clara," he said. "You're my best friend. If you can't fall apart on me, then who can you fall apart on anyway?"*

*"I don't even know why I did it," I complained. "Jonathan is a very nice man with a nice house. But I don't love him."*

*"Then don't marry him," he said adamantly. "If it feels wrong, then it is probably wrong."*

*"I have to. I told Papa I would and he's insistent. And I have a dress and everything."*

*"And you always do everything you're told, right?"*

*I nodded miserably.*

*Donald nodded, too. "Well, I have seen the wrath of your papa. The day he came over to our farm, he was so angry he shot at our house and broke the window."*

*"What?" I cried, shocked.*

*Donald told me it was all his mother could do not to call the police. They had stopped because of me, not wanting to leave me on the farm alone. Papa must be under a lot of stress and tension, but even I hadn't known it was that bad.*

*October 20, 1921*

*Oh, things are just terrible. They could not get any worse. My stomach is miserable and aches something awful. At breakfast, I tried broaching the subject of calling off the wedding and Papa grew so furious, he actually threw his plate up against the wall, shouted at me, and stormed out of the house. He must have gone to town because he's not on the farm and it's very late at night now.*

*That's not even the worst of it, not by a long shot. I did something horrid.*

*After Papa left, I went to the clearing and there was Donald, reading. I have no idea what came over me but, without thinking, I ran to him, threw myself into his lap, and buried my face in his neck. Before I knew what was happening, we were melting into the sweetest, most promising kiss I have ever known. Jonathan has kissed me, of course, but those have been quick, hasty, and almost hard. This one was hopeful. I didn't want it to stop and, indeed, I think time stood still!*

*When we were finished he rocked me back and forth for what seemed like an eternity and then, again, I embarrassed myself and cried a little bit. I have gotten myself into such a mess. I wish my mama was still alive.*

*October 28, 1921*

*I am leading two separate lives now. One is full of dress fittings, wedding plans, and looking at menus. I go out with Jonathan and his friends, I visit with his mother and father, I listen to him and Papa talk about business, and I smile at his endless talks of the railroad. I scrub our house from top to bottom, straightening rugs and polishing silver. I mend clothes and sweep the porch. I*

200

cook dinner and breakfast every day. I am even trying to learn how to be a wife.

And in my other life, I sneak away every afternoon to the woods. There, I run through the trees and dance in the sunlight. I read books and sigh over passages that sing to me. I laugh and dream and love and kiss and lay in the arms of the one I really love. I have memorized his every move, his texture, his skin, his hair, his fingernails. I can breathe him. I think, in a blackened room without any sound, I would still know he was there.

I don't know how I am going to live without him.

*November 10, 1921*

Today I overheard an argument between Papa and Jonathan. It was about the oil wells. Oh, I do not think that there are any on our property at all. Jonathan still thinks there are, of course, but he asked Papa for proof of his business contract with the drilling company and Papa grew belligerent. Jonathan stormed out of the house in a rage. Now I wonder if he only wants to marry me because of the wells. What if Papa has lied to him? Is money all anyone cares about anymore? I feel ill.

Jonathan is going out of town on business the day after tomorrow. He won't return for three weeks.

I am going to speak to Papa about Donald tonight.

# Chapter 13

Taryn paced the room impatiently, first sipping on her Coke and then draining it while she waited for Matt to finish reading the pages she had uploaded to him. Allison Moorer sang in the background, something about a soft place to fall. She hadn't trusted going to the library and scanning them; instead, she had taken pictures of them and sent them to his email. It felt like it was taking him forever, but it was less than half an hour. Matt was a fast reader.

"Well." It was a statement.

"Well!?" she pounced.

"I guess we can come up with some theories then, can't we?" he mused thoughtfully.

"So I reckon we can assume poor Donald probably didn't make it out of Vidalia, for starters," she agreed, getting settled on the bed. She'd been dying to talk to him since she finished reading the pages in the heat of her car. She hadn't even been able to make it back to her room before diving into them.

"Not necessarily," he hedged.

"Oh, come on Matt," she snorted. "One of them obviously killed him. Either her dad did it because she was fooling around with him and would have called off the wedding, or Jonathan did it because she would have called off the wedding and either way it would have screwed up their oil deal—the deal that would have made both of them rich. Donald didn't make it out of there alive and one of them is behind it."

"There is another alternative, Taryn. You're always seeing conspiracy theories," Matt chastised. She hated that tone in his voice. It grated on her, although it was true she saw conspiracy theories a lot.

"And what, pray tell, would that be?"

"Maybe he left because he couldn't stand to wait around and watch something he couldn't have," he replied softly.

Even Taryn wasn't dense enough to catch the hitch in his voice and she felt guilty enough to drop her head and bite her lip. It wasn't time, not yet. It might be the right time, maybe one day. But she would know, wouldn't she? If it was meant to be Matt?

"I still think one of them killed her," she said stubbornly.

"So why was the engagement called off?"

"Whose?"

"Maizie's."

"Because she was a bitch, obviously," Taryn snorted. "And then Jonathan got back together with her because men eventually go back to women like that because they're nuts. Maybe he did have a moment of lucidity with Clara but then she died and in a moment of weakness he went back to the crazy chick."

"Your mind confuses me," Matt sighed.

"But I still don't think Clara died of TB. Or consumption. Or anything like it. I think Robert killed her, too. Or maybe Jonathan. Or, hell, maybe Maizie did. But something happened the night she told her dad about Donald because she obviously never wrote about it again. Or anything."

"You just assume everyone was murdered," Matt teased her.

"Well, what do you think?"

"I think we're getting a story from a narrator we can't trust," he replied honestly. "All we know are her thoughts. Maybe there wasn't a deal with the oil well at all. Maybe she thought she overheard something she didn't. Maybe everyone had her good intentions at heart, but her emotions clouded her judgment and reasoning."

"That could be true," Taryn conceded.

"With that being said," he continued. "I agree there is probably foul play here. As to who killed who and when, however, I'm still not sure. But I think we can eliminate Jonathan as an antagonist because it seems he was out of town when everything happened."

"Which leaves us with Robert killing Donald to keep the marriage on and then...well, what happened to Clara?"

Matt sighed. "You got me. Could she have been so lonely she couldn't have seen another way out and followed close behind?"

The thought of Clara snuffing out her own bright candle was somehow more chilling than the image of either man doing it for her.

It took two days to finish the painting and during that time, Taryn didn't have any other incidents at the house. In fact, there was eeriness in that nothing occurred at all. She visited the diner once during that time and was touched to see Tammy's concern over her health. Apparently, her stay at the hospital and the poisoning made the local paper.

"Oh, anything bigger than a parking ticket around here makes the news," Tammy nodded. "You're lucky Janine wasn't running into your room with a camera, trying to get you on the cover."

Remembering how pale she'd been, and the fact that she hadn't seen a hairbrush until she got back to her hotel room, she was glad Janine stayed away. She was sure everyone else in town was glad, too. The last thing she needed was for everyone to see her in all of her natural glory.

"Have you had any more weird stuff out there at the house since the last time I saw you?" Tammy asked conversationally as she delivered Taryn's order of a grilled cheese and peanut butter milkshake. She decided that the weight loss really wasn't working for her after all.

"Well, a little here and there," she conceded. Now wasn't the time to talk about old diaries and murder mysteries. "But listen, do you know any Fitzgeralds?"

"Sure, there's a few around here. I went to school with one. She'd be the granddaughter, great-granddaughter? Something like that. One of the ones who lived in the big house that got torn down, the one up by Windwood Farm. Susan was her name. Her family's still around here. But they never lived in the house, though. That was the daughter, not the son, um..."

"Jonathan?" Taryn supplied.

"Right, Jonathan," Tammy agreed. "It wasn't his kids. He had some but they all moved off. Ohio, Missouri. Something like that. This is his sister's family. And then there are some other Fitzgeralds around. I don't really know them that well. Just the name. But I know they're related to that family, too. The name doesn't mean what it used to, if you know what I'm saying."

"I know what you're saying," Taryn agreed. "Well, while I'm giving you the third degree, what about oil wells? Were there any around here? Was there any drilling?"

"Oh, yeah, all over the county. Back in the 1920s, 1930s, back then. For a long time there was. Not here, not in Vidalia, but in other parts of Stokes County. I had to learn about that in school. They kind of make a big deal about that around here, that and the railroad."

Taryn finished her milkshake and decided it was time to take a trip back to the Stokes County Historical Society.

There were only two ladies present when she walked in that Saturday afternoon: Phyllis, the bird-woman, and the president, Geneva. Both were silently working on computers when she let herself into the doublewide and jumped a little when the door slammed behind her.

"Good Lord, child," Phyllis cried as she turned around and peered over her wiry glasses. "You're about to give an old woman a heart attack. I was so lost in thought, I think I went back in time a little bit."

"I'm sorry about that," Taryn apologized. "I didn't realize it would be so loud."

"Us old folks scare easily," Geneva laughed, as she ushered Taryn into the room and pointed her to a chair. "How are you feeling, dear? You look an awful lot better than you did the last time! An awful lot."

"Now the girl doesn't want to hear that, Geneva," Phyllis admonished. "It wasn't so bad, child, although you were a bit peaked. You do look lovely today, though. So fresh and young."

"I feel a whole lot better, I can tell you that much," she admitted. "I'm going to work on the frame tomorrow and Monday and I think I can have the painting delivered to you by Tuesday afternoon, if that's okay."

"Oh," Phyllis clapped her small hands together. "That would be perfect. I am so excited. Aren't you excited, Geneva?"

"As a rose after a rainstorm!" she cried. "I just can't wait to see it. I bet it's beautiful."

"I actually came here to ask you a couple of questions, though. I thought you might be able to help me with a few things."

"Well, we can surely try," Phyllis smiled pleasantly. She wore a thin cotton dress and bright pink sneakers. Her knee-highs had fallen down and were pooled around her wrinkled ankles, but her white cotton candy hair was in an intricate chignon that Taryn imagined a professional had done for her.

"Can you tell me anything about the oil wells here in Vidalia?"

"Oh," Geneva waved her hand dismissively. "There are a few around here, but none have ever been drilled. Now, there were some over in Fitz that made a lot of people a lot of money at one time, right Phyllis?"

Phyllis laughed. "Oh, yes, those wells. The oil and the railroad. But no, dear, there aren't any in Vidalia. At least not any that have ever been touched."

"So there aren't any at Windwood Farm then?" she asked, trying to sound casual. She wasn't ready to share her find yet with anyone. She didn't know why, but the story didn't feel finished and she wanted to keep it to herself until she had more answers.

"Not that I'm aware of," Geneva answered. "Why? Did you find one? Because that might be a coup for Reagan when he starts his demolition."

*Oh, yeah*, Taryn thought. *He might find a lot of things when he starts that demolition.* But she kept her mouth shut. "No, I just wondered. I heard about there being a lot in the area and I just thought that maybe..." Not just how to end the sentence she just let it die off.

"Not that I never knew of," Geneva answered. "If there had been one, you could've bet that he'd been trying to get it out of the ground some way at least, what with the money he owed."

Taryn chewed on this. It left an unanswered question. Why hadn't he tried to find a way to get to the oil even after her death, if it had really been there? Unless, of course, there really hadn't been any oil to start with?

"How would that have worked anyway, if someone had one on their property?"

"Well, generally they would have sold the rights to a company and that company would have done the drilling. The individual might have sold their property or the mineral rights, it just depended on how fancy the company did the talking," Phyllis smiled.

"Kind of like coal mining?" Taryn asked.

"You could say that," Phyllis agreed. "An oil well won't produce forever, but it will for a good long time and if the field is good, they might find more than one site, especially on a farm. Something like that was good not only for that farm, but for the ones around it, too. Increased local property values."

"But you couldn't lie about something like that, right? I mean, not to the drilling companies."

"Not for long anyway," Geneva chuckled. "They'd eventually find that there wasn't any oil. Might get by with lying to your neighbors, but not to the machines."

Luckily, the other women changed the subject at that time and began talking about the Great Depression and World War II, so she was saved by any further questions from them. It did set some other wheels in motion, though.

"**W**ow, that's amazing."

The voice came from behind Taryn and startled her so much that she almost dropped the brush. She didn't even hear a car approaching or anyone get out of it. Sometimes she got in the zone but she knew she wasn't *that* out of it. Turning around at the sound of Melissa's voice, Taryn smiled. "Hey, I didn't hear you come up."

"Sorry, I walked. It's not that bad of a walk, really. Just through the woods there. About half an hour and it gets me out of the house. I do it every few days," she shrugged.

*Just like Donald did,* Taryn thought with cold chills.

"So, what do you think?" she asked, stepping back from the easel and crossing her arms over her chest. She didn't normally have an audience this early on.

"I think it's incredible, I really do. It must have been a beautiful house when all of it was still here."

"Yeah, it must have been," Taryn agreed. Too bad it was filled with sadness, death, and probably murder.

"Listen, after talking to you a few weeks ago, I talked to my aunt and she had some stories to tell me, about my family. I wanted to pass them on to you because of the interest you had in them, about Donald."

Taryn was starting to feel a little guilty about not telling Melissa of the diary she'd discovered, but the hairs on her arms were starting to rise and it was a feeling she didn't normally ignore.

"Okay, but let me just put this away first and let's go sit down, all right? I've had some trouble lately and I don't want to have to start from scratch, you know?"

It didn't take long for her to stick the canvas in the back of her car. For good measure, she locked her doors. She couldn't leave it in there long, the heat wasn't good for it, but her windows were tinted and she was parked under a tree. It would be fine for a while.

Moving over to the house, they found places on the front porch and Taryn offered Melissa an Ale-8. She would miss those when she was gone. She wondered how many she could fit in her trunk before she left.

"Ahhh," Melissa sighed as she took a swig. "Nothing like an ice cold one of these on a hot day. "The nectar of the gods."

"So, what you got for me?"

"Maybe not much," Melissa shrugged. "But supposedly a few months before he disappeared there was a big fight between his dad and the owner of this farm. He even shot out their window or something. Donald even got involved in it. It was messy. I guess the owner here didn't let it go, either, and showed up there a few more times, threatening them. He owed them money, legit and everything, and then refused to pay it. But he got all paranoid about it, like they were trying to harass him to get it back. From what I understand, though, they'd just let it go because they were scared of him."

"So did they think someone else was harassing him and making him think it was them?"

211

"Nah," Melissa snorted. "They just thought he was nuts. My aunt said that people in Vidalia thought the daughter here was real sweet, shy as a church mouse, but a nice kid. She was engaged to the man on the other side."

"I know all about that," Taryn nodded. "Listen, I have to tell you something, too. I have reason to think that Donald did not just walk away from here. You see, the other day when I was here I found this—"

Before she even finished the sentence, a wail so long and deep it made both women drop their bottles to the ground shook through the house. "You heard that, right?" Melissa whispered.

Taryn nodded and then shot through the door and up the stairs, one thing on her mind: Clara. She had to know what had happened. "Clara!" she called. "Clara! Don't go!"

With Melissa on her heels, she burst through the bedroom door, only to realize she had forgotten Miss Dixie below. "Shit, shit. A phone, a phone. Do you have your phone on you?"

The crying was fainter now, but still shook through the walls, reverberating through the women's soles of their shoes and up their legs. "Wha—" Melissa fumbled through her pocket until she found it.

"Take a picture," Taryn cried. "The bed! Take a picture!" It just felt right.

Melissa snapped a shot of the bed, but it came away empty.

"Okay, it has to be Dixie, shit!" Taryn cried. "I don't think I have time. The crying's stopping. Or maybe it has to me me. Here," she reached for the phone and aimed it at the bed. With a single press of the thumb, the sounds stopped.

Both women gasped.

"Holy mother of God," Melissa whispered.

"Jesus Christ," Taryn breathed.

Again, the very faint outline of a young woman lay on the rumpled bed. But the this time, her arms were raised above her head, neatly wrapped in chains and bound to the wrought iron posts behind her.

It was getting dark when she pulled into the deserted parking lot, but the "open" sign was still on in the small shop, giving her hope. This time, when she went inside, she went straight to the counter and didn't hesitate.

"I need help," she said simply.

Rob, she had taken time to learn his name on her last visit, was wearing a Metallica T-shirt today and was busy trying to fix the screen on an iPhone. "Hey, what's up?" One look at her face, however, told him most of what he needed to know.

"It either went very well, or really, really badly," he said sympathetically, putting down the tools and giving her his full attention.

"Well," she agreed, raking her hands through her hair and leaning up against the counter. "It depends on how you look at it. But I need answers and nobody can give them to me."

"You want to know what happened in the house?" he asked.

"No. Well, yes, but I think I'm figuring that out. I want to know what's happening with *me*," she said, and was embarrassed to find that tears were actually starting to form in her eyes. "Shit."

Rob quickly got up and moved out from behind the counter. Despite the fact that a young couple was heading toward the shop, he flipped off the "open" sign and waved them away. "If it's important, they'll come back," he muttered as he walked back to Taryn. "Okay, come back here, sit down, and tell me what's going on."

He had somewhat of an office behind the counter and she was surprised to find comfortable overstuffed chairs, a flat screen television, a panel of computer screens, an almost feminine bordello lamp, and a coffee table with what looked like an antique teapot. "I like to get cozy and work at the same time," he explained. "Tea?"

"Sure, why not?"

She waited while he put the water on to boil using a hot plate he kept stashed behind the counter. It was cinnamon-flavored and the warmth of the lamp and scent of the tea when he poured it into her cup was enough to relax her. Almost.

"So tell me what's going on with you," he prodded. "Did the ritual not work?"

"Oh, I think it did," she answered and told him about finding the diary. "The story's a tragic one and a bad one and I feel awful about it. I haven't completely pieced it together yet, but I'm

214

working on it. But I want to know why? Why now? Why me? Why is this happening?"

"Taryn," he said gently. "These kinds of things rarely happen overnight. I can't think this is the first experience you've had with the paranormal."

Remembering that afternoon in the empty house as a child, she shuddered. "No, it's not. There were little things along the way, of course, and I've always been a little sensitive to people's feelings and emotions. But nothing like this. I even thought it was my camera, like maybe it was magic." They both laughed a little.

"But it's you," he said.

"It's me."

"When you see the visions through the camera, do you ever see them outside? Like, when your camera isn't on?"

"No," she replied. "Not since I was little. I can hear things, sometimes, but I haven't really seen anything yet. Nothing more than a shadow, anyway. And it might have been a trick of the sun."

"Hmmm..." He studied her thoughtfully. "And these energy forces—that's what we'll call them—can you interact with them? Do they know you're there? Can you speak to them?"

"I've tried to talk to them but I don't know if they're reacting to me or not. I thought they were. Maybe the negative one is. But Clara? No. She doesn't respond. I don't think she knows I'm there at all. It's just like looking at a picture. Or hearing something on television."

The tea felt nice on her stomach and sitting here, far away from Windwood Farm and her hotel room, she even felt a little silly about the whole thing. But then she remembered the vision of poor little Clara chained up to the bed and the look of utter grief on her face and she shook her head again, trying to shake it away.

"I should be happy, right? I have dedicated my life to the past. I studied the architecture, the history, the stories. I help people try to see it. And now, I *can* see it. It should be a dream come true, right?"

"There are people who would pay for such gifts," he agreed. "But I think every gift comes with a price. Taryn, how old are you?"

"I turned thirty last February."

"The end of the month?" he asked. She nodded.

"That might make more sense then. You're a Pisces, a water sign. Those signs tend to be more sensitive to these kinds of things. And, well, the 30th birthday is a big one. I haven't seen your astrological chart, but I reckon if we pulled one up on you, we'd see a lot of change in your life. You might have moved into a new phase and with that phase, had these new doors open for you."

"Do you believe that? That I woke up and had special gifts?"

"No," he laughed. "I think everyone has them, to an extent, anyway. But there might be more to it than your age and your sign. Is there anything else in the house that might have attracted you, Taryn?" he asked gently.

"What do you mean?"

"This young woman who died, her story? Do you feel a pull to it?"

Taryn looked down at her feet, the beginning of a headache tugging behind her eyes. "Maybe. I guess. My fiancé. He passed away in a car accident several years ago. He was driving...he liked to drive fast. Used to brag about breaking the speed limit. It was raining, the road was curvy, he was coming home late from a job site. I was sick and wasn't with him."

"Then it's possible that the energy in this house, with this young woman who may have died with a love in her life, is picking up on your grief, too," Rob said softly. "If you still haven't gotten closure."

"I don't know. It's possible. I feel connected to Clara. I don't know why. When I read her diary, I almost...envied her," she finished lamely.

"Your fiancé, was he the love of your life, your soul mate?"

"Yes, I thought so at the time," she replied honestly. "He was my best friend, my other half. We shared everything together, even work. He was a much better person than I am. But now, the grief and loneliness has clouded so much I just don't—*can't* remember."

The two of them sat in silence for several minutes before Taryn spoke again. "So you think everyone has sensitivities? Do you?"

"I can't see the past like you can, but I have an audible sensitivity most others don't. I can hear certain things almost miles away. If my mother is coughing, for instance, on the other side of town or my sister cries out in the night in another state from a bad dream, I can hear it. It sounds like they're in the room with me. It's not a developed gift and I can't control it, but it's there."

"Matt doesn't have anything like that and I've known him almost my whole life," she mused.

"Oh, I wouldn't say that. After spending almost five years in college with the dude and his mega brain, I can assure you there is half a university that thinks he has some kind of strange powers, the way his mind can soak up information and retain it. People's gifts come in all shapes and sizes. This might just be yours. Maybe this was why you were called to Historical Preservation and why you're such a fine artist."

"Because it's like, my calling?" The thought, for some reason, gave her chills.

"Who knows?" he shrugged. "What you do with it is up to you. But Taryn, I don't think it's going away. As a matter of fact, I think it's going to get stronger."

# Chapter 14

So that was it. She was going to have to learn to live with the spirits and whatever she saw and prepare for the fact that things might get worse in the future. Whatever she was scared of as a child was only the tip of the iceberg of what she would be exposed to as an adult.

Awesome.

And poor Clara. Well, she could only guess what had happened to *her*. Obviously, her father killed her. Probably horribly. And he'd probably had something to do with Donald's death, too. Melissa agreed and they parted that afternoon, both shaken and subdued. How guilty was Jonathan in the whole mess? She didn't know. Had he come back to find his new almost-wife dead or had he had a hand in it himself when he'd learned of her betrayal? Taryn might never know.

The painting was finished, however, and as she slicked the last coat of varnish over the frame, she felt that at least one part of her job was complete. In most cases, she would have moved on and gone to the next job. This would become a memory, an anecdote to tell other clients about in the future. In fact, she'd already taken on a new project, a historical library in Missouri. She would start in two weeks, giving her plenty of time to recuperate in Nashville.

But she wasn't ready to leave yet. She knew she wasn't finished.

While she waited for the varnish to dry, Taryn sat on her bed and flipped through the pictures on her computer screen once again. She had hundreds of shots of Windwood Farm, but this time, she went back to the first ones she'd taken; those pictures she had snapped when she first arrived on the job.

Her bags were already packed and the only things left out were what she would need in the morning when she got dressed. She planned on doing one more diner run for pancakes and a milkshake and thought she might stop off and tell Melissa goodbye. Seemed a cold way to leave someone, really. "Hey, your ancestor was murdered and might be buried somewhere on these grounds. See ya later!" She should at least take her some chocolate. And the diary. After all, it wasn't Taryn's.

The first pictures of the house's interior still gave her a start. Seeing the furniture that wasn't supposed to be there gave her chills even now, despite everything that had happened since.

But it was the very first picture that caught her eye this time. It was of the outside of the house. She'd looked at it a dozen times, especially when she was working late at night and needed inspiration or some of the detail work. It wasn't a great shot, at least in terms of composition, but it gave her a good view of the entire front. But why hadn't she noticed that object in the front yard before? It wasn't large, and it was partly obstructed by the debris from the collapsed part of the house, but it was definitely there. At least, it was there in the image. It wasn't there *now*. She'd stood in that same spot countless times, had even laid there and felt the grass on her face, but not once had she noticed a well. But here, in this image, it was as plain as day. The old spigot, the stone wall...a little rise in the ground almost hid it, and she enlarged the image now to see it better, but there it was: right below Clara's window.

"Holy hell," she whispered. "I'll be damned."

Jumping up off the bed, she threw on her boots and a long-sleeved shirt and grabbed her keys, cellphone, and camera. It might have been in the middle of the night, but she couldn't wait until morning. She had to know *now*.

Of course, the debris of the house covered most of the spot where the well would have been. There were certainly no signs of it now. The round ring of rocks, where she had fallen on one of her first days there, wasn't anywhere near where she thought the well was. That theory had gone out the window.

Her headlights illuminated the front of the house and, camera in hand, she marched around, taking pictures as quickly as she could. The bright flash lit up the sky like little lightning bolts. Still, her LCD screen showed nothing but grass.

"I *know* it was here," she sighed in frustration. "Why is it not showing up?"

In exasperation, she sat down on the ground and put her head in her hands. "I was so close," she cried, discouraged. "I really thought I could do this."

The house and yard were quiet, not even a tree frog chirped in the night. It would've been a great time for one of the spirits to have made themselves known or to have given her a sign. Everyone in town talked about how scary the place was and here she was, out there alone by herself in the middle of the night. But there was nothing.

She was rising to her feet and getting ready to give it up and go back to the hotel when she suddenly felt a hard, heavy object hit the side of her head. The last thing she thought as she fell over to the ground was, *Well, I didn't see that one coming.*


Taryn woke up to the sensation of being dragged. She felt her body moving along the ground as the dry grass scraped at her cheeks. Someone was tugging on her feet. She had the distinct awareness of feeling grateful that no rain had fallen in the past 24 hours, or else the ground would've been wet and she would've had grass stains on her jeans. It was a crazy thought, but it was also a crazy situation. When she tried to open her eyes to see who was pulling on her, however, she found her eyelids too heavy. *Maybe I'll just go back to sleep*, she thought. The pain on the side of her head was dull and throbbing.

She was only dragged for a couple of feet before the culprit abruptly dropped her legs to the ground. She could hear them walking away and even in her state, Taryn knew that was the time to act. *Gotta get up*, she thought. *Gotta get moving before the bad guy comes back with a chainsaw or something.*

Trying to ignore the pain in her head, she rolled over to her side and rose to her knees. It was still dark out and she could still see her car, although the headlights were off. So she was still at Windwood Farm. She couldn't see anyone else, however. Feeling in her pocket, she found her car keys and tried to judge how quickly she could make a run for it. It was only about fifty feet away, but she didn't know what or who waited for her in the darkness.

As she jumped to her feet, however, she heard the cock of a gun. "I wouldn't do that if I were you," came a thin, reedy voice.

Taryn knew the gun was pointed at her and as the figure stepped into the moonlight, the shadow of the house silhouetted behind her, she was only mildly surprised to see the bird-woman.

"You're not really going to shoot me, are you, Phyllis?" she asked conversationally, still fingering her keys.

"I don't want to—too messy—but if you leave me no choice, dear, then I might have to. If I'd been a little younger, that shovel would've knocked you plumb out and done a lot worse, and I wouldn't be worrying with you now," she said plaintively.

"Well, it was still a pretty good hit," Taryn reasoned. "It knocked me out and my head still hurts." She had no idea why she was trying to make this mad woman feel better about trying to kill her.

"You weren't supposed to come out here tonight. In a few minutes, my son will be here and he'll take care of you," she whined. "Why are you here so late? It's too damn dark to paint!"

223

"I forgot something," Taryn lied and found herself almost on the verge of apologizing. "I had to come back."

The bird-woman shook her head. "We know that's not true. I know you've figured out what happened here, and what happened to my uncle. Poor Uncle Jonathan. He should never have gotten messed up with them folks. They ruined him, they did. He loved that little girl, Lord knows why. Would've done anything to marry her. Even had her daddy believing there was a gas well on here just so he could have her. Said he'd make him a rich man. He told my mama that on his death bed. There weren't no gas wells here, of course. But that old fool didn't know it. He was greedy, wanted money. He'd believe anything."

Taryn was taken aback. So it was just a lie? And Jonathan really had feelings for Clara? Well, that was different. She'd been wrong.

"But Jonathan didn't kill her, Phyllis. He had nothing to do with it," she reasoned again. "And it happened a long time ago."

"What's time," Phyllis snapped. "Nobody forgets. And I won't have you dragging my family's name in the mud. No, he didn't kill her. And when Robert told him what he'd done to that other boy and that she'd died, he went out of his mind with grief. He was a good man, my uncle. Tried to make things right."

"All towns have a haunted house, Phyllis, it's just for fun. It's part of their history. It's nothing personal," she tried again.

"You say that when it's part of *your* history," she snapped. "You're dragging my family through the mud! Uncle Jonathan would have married that girl and her no good daddy would've gotten out of debt. But he went insane. Did what he did and my uncle couldn't help it. It was all over greed. Uncle Jonathan told him that if he ever tried to drill and get another oil company involved, he'd bring the authorities right to that well, even if it meant that his name got dragged in the mud right along with it. He didn't care! He was a good man. He tried to make things right in the end and hoped everyone would forget. And they did! Until you come around."

Taryn wanted to ask what she meant, thinking that stalling was her best option, but Phyllis' agitation was becoming more pronounced.

"I won't tell anyone. Nobody even *knows*, Phyllis. Believe me, they don't. I've asked everyone. They just think this house is haunted, they don't know the story behind it."

Phyllis snorted. "You've been all over town asking questions. Everyone knows. And how do you think I feel, having this house and this place like a freak show, a carnival ride? Right next to my family homestead? It's a joke! How long until they put it together and my family's name is dragged through the mud? My son's here to dig up that well. We know what's down there and you do, too. He knows about you, too. Was his idea for the tea and the tires. We thought maybe it would be enough. But you're ornery."

Taryn felt prickles of pride that she knew were silly. She tried to take a step back. "Just let me go home. Take whatever is in that well and I'll leave and forget about it."

"I'd like to, of course. I don't want no death on my hands. I'm a good, *Christian* woman. But when you die, your family's

225

name is all you got left. When my mama told me our secret, I promised to take it to my grave. And that means taking it to yours, too."

They both heard the car turning into the drive at the same time. Taryn screamed and lunged at Phyllis the same time she decided to pull the trigger. As the bullet raced through her shoulder and Taryn felt the ground under her once again, she just hoped the son wouldn't be too hard on her or as sadistic as some of the killers on the crime shows she liked to watch.


Once again, Taryn found herself waking up to bright lights and the soft sounds of voices. Both her head and shoulder hurt, but she also felt a little floaty and drowsy and it was nice. She couldn't be on the ground anymore because the surface under her felt too soft. And her jeans were gone. She knew because she could feel her bare legs. The material under her was a little scratchy, a little cottony. She was too uncomfortable for this to be Heaven, though.

"Hey," came a soft female voice. "You're awake! Look at you!"

On experiment, Taryn tried opening her eyes and was amazed to find herself back in the same hospital room. Melissa sat at her side, a carton of apple juice in her hand. "Sorry, but I drank your juice. You didn't look like you'd be wanting it and my mouth was really, really dry. It's still hot out there."

"Hey, I'm not dead," Taryn smiled. "What the hell happened?"

"Reagan got the voicemail you left him before you left the hotel. He decided to come out and check things for himself. Be glad you're in Kentucky where men carry guns in their trucks or else you might be dead. We heard the shot on our farm, too, and my husband was heading over. He got there the same time as Phyllis's son and the police. They've both been arrested. It's kind of sad, really."

Taryn nodded. "And so pointless. Does reputation really mean so much? I mean, for people who have been dead for so long?"

"I guess so. Heritage is a big deal. People want to protect it," Melissa explained. "It was Phyllis's life, apparently. She didn't want her family associated with something so horrible. She was afraid you'd bring it all out into the open."

They both stayed in companionable silence until Taryn broke it again. "I hoped they liked the painting, anyway."

Melissa giggled. "Oh, and I talked to your friend Matt. I got in touch with him on your phone. I hope that's okay."

Taryn nodded. "Thank you. He would've killed me a second time. Or third. Whatever. I've lost count."

"He came up with something on his own. He did his own research and guess what he found? Until the house sold, Jonathan Fitzgerald paid the taxes and kept the house up. So he must have really loved Clara."

"Or at least felt responsible for what happened," Taryn added. "And no wonder. A combination of his greed, Robert's greed, and Robert's lies killed two people."

"Well, maybe…Some of it might not have been lies. They found Donald's body in the well. Reagan had them dig it up. Nobody even knew it was there. Of course, it's just bones now. But we know it's his. We won't know until they do a bunch of testing, but who else? There was a lock on that well, too, an old one. Police figured it's been on there since the '20s."

"I bet I know where the key is that fits the lock," Taryn murmured.

"And guess what else they found?" Melissa added.

"What?"

"Oil wells. In the back."

Taryn's eyes grew large. "Holy shit! They've been busy."

"No kidding! Reagan's got that place torn apart. Robert wasn't lying. Of course, he might not have known he wasn't lying at the time, but yeah, they were really there all along. They **all** would have been rich," Melissa said a little sadly. "Well, the Fitzgeralds were already rich, but they would have been even richer. That should have made them happy. That's what Jonathan wanted all along. To be richer."

Taryn closed her eyes and thought about poor Donald, going to see Clara. For what? Had they decided to run away together? Was he going to ask Robert for permission to finally be with her? Or was he just concerned and checking on her? "We'll never know how Donald died. But I have theories. My worst one is he simply threw him into the well and Clara, tied to the bed, had to listen to him drown or scream until he died."

Melissa shuddered. "That's mine, too. I'm hoping maybe the bones show a gunshot wound or something. I don't know if that's possible. But she had to know he was dead. Do you think he killed her, too?"

"I don't think so. In her diary she talked about her stomach hurting, feeling pale, and not being able to eat but feeling hungry. I'd say that under all that stress she worked herself up a good old-fashioned stomach ulcer. I believe she died from complications of it, or she vomited blood and choked on it. The coroner probably couldn't tell the difference, especially with the blood on the sheets and her mother's history of TB."

"So he did kill her, just in a different way," Melissa said unhappily. "So many lives ruined. I heard that Jonathan married that woman Maizie he used to see and they were never that happy. She was a weird, cold woman."

"And poor little Clara's life was snuffed out before it even got started," Taryn added.

Melissa nodded sadly.

"So Phyllis's uncle is going to be tied into an eighty-year old murder case and Donald will finally get the burial he deserves. But what about Clara? Who cares about her and what happened?"

"I do," Melissa said, a touch of stubbornness showing through. "I care about her. And my family will, too. She's our family now. We'll take care of her. I've already visited her grave and I'll keep doing it. We'll make sure she's not forgotten."

Despite the awkwardness, the members of the Stokes County Historical Society loved the painting. A few even openly cried when they saw it. As they walked around the room and hugged and patted on her, she felt both pride and embarrassment at their displays of affection.

Shirley seemed particularly upset. "I am just so sorry that...so sorry. I'm sorry that—"

"One of your members tried to kill me?" Taryn finished helpfully. "Twice?

That seemed to break the spell and put everyone at ease, although Taryn couldn't wait to get out of the building and Vidalia itself. She still wasn't sure why the well hadn't shown up in her last pictures, but she knew that the part that centered on her wasn't finished. She might have known what happened to Clara, but her story was really just beginning. Rob was right. She had changed. She felt it. Something was starting to unfold inside of her and awaken. It was a prickling at the edges of her mind, but she couldn't ignore it. In the hospital, after the attack, it grew stronger. She itched to take more pictures and see what developed, no pun intended.

There wasn't much left to say goodbye to. Taryn stood awkwardly in the middle of her hotel room, taking one last look around. The mirror over the standard, hotel dresser showed a reflection of a woman who, to Taryn's mind anyway, looked older and more tired than she was when she'd first arrived. Taryn felt like she'd aged by at least ten years over the past six weeks. "Probably the Pine Sol," she joked aloud and her voice felt dim and hollow in the empty room.

Nobody knew what happened to the mirror in Clara's room. Not every question was answered in the end. Perhaps a vandal really *had* taken it sometime over the years. Or maybe one of the other owners removed it. Taryn liked to think that Robert, left alone with his anger and whatever madness he had inside of him, removed the mirror himself because he felt Clara's spirit wandering through the house.

Reagan gave the keys to Melissa. Nobody spoke of them aloud, but they all knew what those keys were for. The smaller ones would have been for the padlocks that held the chains on Clara's bed. And the larger key fit the door that covered the old well once it was uncovered. Had Robert left the keys there for Clara to see, so close and yet unable to reach them? What would drive a person to be so insane? No amount of criminal shows on television could help Taryn reach that level of understanding. Her own parents were aloof and distant, but they loved her. Maybe, in his own way, Robert also loved his daughter. Had his debts pushed him into believing that keeping her tied down and forcing her to marry someone she didn't love was the only way out for him? Obviously, Taryn didn't really know them, but if he had talked to Clara she had a feeling that Clara's sense of duty to her family would have pushed her into the marriage if nothing else. His actions had been senseless, pointless. She wondered what he was like when his wife was still alive. So many questions left unanswered but at least the living knew the answers to the most important questions and that would have to be enough.

Taryn made one last stop at the diner for pancakes before leaving town. Tammy was waiting for her when she walked in and immediately pounced on her with a hug. "I don't care if you're not the touchy type, you're getting one," she said into Taryn's shoulder.

"I'm the hugging type and I probably need one about now," she sighed and then realized she would really miss the meals and companionship she found there.

"I'm sorry we tried to kill you. Twice." Tammy looked so forlorn that Taryn couldn't help but laugh as she slid into the booth.

"Well, I can't say this is one job that I am going to miss. But I will miss you. And the food."

"I'm taking a break," Tammy called into the kitchen. A grumble of noises came back out and Tammy waved them away as she slid in across from Taryn. "Nobody else here, anyway. Breakfast rush is over."

Taryn was still sore and figured that she'd have nightmares for years over what had happened, like she needed any more reasons not to be able to sleep. She hadn't been back out to the house since the night she went looking for the well. Part of her wanted to go, just to see if the air changed. The other part was too afraid of what she might see, or not see.

"Do you think it's over?" Tammy asked, as if reading her mind.

It took Taryn a second to realize she was talking about Windwood Farm and not what she had been experiencing through her camera. "I don't know. Maybe. Maybe Clara's soul can rest now, and Donald's. I don't know about the other. With new people and new houses and a new lease on life, the property might just bounce back from this."

"And it might not," Tammy added.

"And it might not," Taryn echoed.

"Who knows," Tammy laughed, the sound filling the diner; a symbol of hope. "The old place might not even let them tear it down!"



The interstate was surprisingly empty as she headed out of Stokes County and pointed her car southbound. It was a clear blue day and even though her shoulder hurt like hell and she'd had to spend a week in the hospital recovering, most of her felt good. The house was going to be demolished sooner rather than later and this time it felt right.

"It's not a good place, Matt," she spoke into her phone. "It might have been at one time, but it's not anymore. It just needs to go. There are just too many bad memories for that house and land. It's time for some happy ones. I hate subdivisions, but maybe once it's filled with families and laughter, the bad energy it's clinging onto will disappear."

"Are *you* okay?" he must have said a thousand prayers for her, and he wasn't even the praying kind. It was the thought of angering her that kept him away this time, but he wouldn't let that hold him back if it happened again.

"I feel good," she said truthfully. "I'm doing something that feels right. I have no idea what this means for me, but I think I'm ready for it."

Coming August 2014

# *Griffith Tavern*

Book Two in Taryn's Camera Series

Visit www.tarynscamera.com

# Acknowledgements

It took a few different people over the course of several years to make this book happen. Thank you to Wanda, Angie, Jennifer, Ginger, and Amy for giving it a read before anyone else. Special thanks to my mom for proofing it for me and catching the weird mistakes, like when I called characters by the wrong name (hey, when it takes you 5 years to write a book, it's bound to happen). Special thanks to Joette Morris Gates who had no idea what she was getting into when I asked her to give it a read and then promptly got hit with approximately 10,000 questions and diligently answered them all. This story was inspired in equal parts by a dream, song lyrics, and a deserted house my husband and I stumbled across one winter's day. I thought my imagination was twisted and then my husband came up with some of the other crazy ideas for the book so as it turns out, we're well-matched after all. Truth can be as strange as fiction: Clara's bedroom actually does exist. Let's hope the real story isn't as crazy as the one in my head. This book is dedicated to one of the most unique and interesting women I have ever known. She encouraged me to write my first ghost story almost 26 years ago. Hopefully, my grammar has improved somewhat. (Some may or may not agree.)

# Sneak Peek at *Griffith Tavern*

## *Griffith Tavern*
Book 2 in Taryn's Camera
Available Now

**I**t was late, but Taryn couldn't sleep. Instead, she'd drawn herself a nice bubble bath. She didn't have any actual bubble bath, but she always took hotel sample shampoos and soaps from her rooms when she traveled and her suitcase was full of them. Emptying out five bottles had produced a nice froth.

She let the water run as hot as she could stand it, Andrew always told people if she couldn't boil a chicken in it then the water wasn't hot enough, and let herself slide. It was quiet. The other guests at the B&B were checking out as she was checking in. Nothing stirred; the only sounds were the soapy bottles crinkling in the water.

*I love my job*, she thought, her mind feeling relaxed and a little mushy. I love being able to wake up every morning, feeling excited about going to work. I love being able to do something I enjoy.

She may have dozed a little. Her arms floated up to the top of the water and rested there, gently bobbing up and down. She knew she should get out, especially when the water turned tepid, but even the idea felt like too much effort.

Suddenly, a slight noise disturbed her reverie. It was a distinct creak from her bedroom and it had her sitting up straight in the water. She cocked her ear towards the sound, straining to listen. Someone was walking around in the room. She knew that creak; she'd been making it all afternoon as she unpacked. The bathroom door was closed almost all the way to, but she was sure a shadow passed before it and another creak in the floorboards confirmed it. She could feel the little hairs on the back of her neck stand at attention. Her arms chilled, goosebumps running up them.

The woman who owned it? "Delphina, is that you?" she called.

With no answer in return, she quickly stood up and wrapped a towel around her.

Feeling naked and vulnerable, Taryn tiptoed to the door, her heart pounding so hard she could see the skin pumping through the towel. The creak came again; this time it sounded like it was close to her dresser. "Who's there?" She hoped her voice wasn't trembling. Despite the fact it sounded as though someone was obviously walking around on her floors, the air was eerily calm and quit. She couldn't detect any breathing.

The closest thing to her was a tall can of shaving cream so she grabbed it and held it over her head, her arm shaking. With her other hand, she clutched at her towel.

Deciding to go at it all at once, like ripping of a Band-Aid, she flung open the bathroom door with her foot, ready to pounce on whoever might be lurking in the darkness.

The room was empty. She was sure she'd left the lamp on the dresser on. Still, even in the dimness she could tell nobody was in there. Her bedroom door was shut and locked from the inside.

"There's nobody here," she muttered. "I really must be going crazy."

But there was a feeling in the air that tugged at her, a feeling that she'd just missed someone. The air currents were still moving, still alive with electricity. She wasn't alone; she knew it. Whoever was there was gone, but there had been someone there.

Stomping over to the dresser, she switched on the bordello style lamp. The light flickered for a moment, like it might not come on, and then the area was illuminated in a sea of gold. She was just about ready to turn around and head back to the bathroom to get her robe when the mirror on the dresser caught her eye. "Oh shit!" she yelped, stumbling backwards and losing her grip on the towel.

The large oval mirror was covered in steam. In its opaqueness she couldn't make out her reflection or the rest of the room in it. In the very center, however, in large letters, the words "Help me" were written in a shaky hand. As she watched in dismay, they slowly faded until the glass was clear and she was staring back at herself, her mouth open in horror.

# About the Author

Rebecca Patrick-Howard is the author of several books including the first book in her paranormal mystery trilogy *Windwood Farm*. She lives in eastern Kentucky with her husband and two children.

Rebecca's other books include:

*Windwood Farm (Book 1 in Taryn's Camera)*

*Four Months of Terror*

*Haunted Estill County*

*More Tales from Haunted Estill County*

*Coping with Grief: The Anti-Guide to Infant Loss*

Visit her website at www.rebeccaphoward.net and sign up for her newsletter to receive free books, special offers, and news.

25257950R00137

Made in the USA
Middletown, DE
23 October 2015